GUARDIANS OF SANCTUARY BOOK 6

ECHOES OF ARCADIA

TL SHIVELY

ECHOES OF ARCADIA

Sanctuary Guardians Book 6

ACKNOWLEDGMENTS

Thank you to all my family and friends, I love you all.

ABOUT THE AUTHOR

TL Shively writes YA fantasy with a twist, including her debut novel, *The Guardians*, and later, the *Spider Trilogy*, which was her own personal challenge to herself, turning her fear of spiders into a story about Gods and Aliens. Fueled by her mother's encouragement and whimsical tales of childhood imaginary friends, she has been crafting stories since grade school. When not working on new stories that explore different realms of fantasy, TL enjoys spending time with her husband, family, and friends, whether playing cornhole or exploring their home state of Michigan.

Ebook: 978-1-952325-19-9
Paperback: 978-1-952325-20-5

Editing by Partners in Crime Book Services
Formatting by Dreams2media

1

Telara watched her twin sister, Tiara, as she slept soundly.
Telara sat quietly atop the dresser in Tiara's room. Her eyes
drifted to the analog clock ticking away the minutes. Their
grandmother gave them each one for their seventh birthday
when they were learning how to read them in school. Solid
oak wood, quartz movement, with a small golden pendulum
that moved back and forth. So much history in this room, her
childhood lived in every detail, a part of her life about to
disappear in mere minutes. She glanced again at the clock;
thirty minutes left.

Ira told them they had until six o'clock Monday morning
after graduation to spend with their families. Originally, it
had been just the morning after graduation, but Ira had
surprisingly fought to give them two extra days. Each of them
spent the weekend with their families, something that caught
their families off guard but they quickly embraced the idea.
Cole spent the weekend in the garage with his dad, working
on the Firebird his father had bought him for graduation.
Black, with a gold phoenix on the hood. His dad had been
saving for years to afford it. Cole had posters of firebirds in
every shape, color, and year that plastered his walls.

Tiara murmured in her sleep, rolling over and throwing her arm off the edge of the bed. Tiara had always been a restless sleeper. Their mom used to tell them how Tiara would always kick Telara when they were babies and sleeping together. Telara looked down at her wrist, at the golden bracelet with the dangling charm; a letter T with a tree overlaid. Tiara wore one with a flower on it. Their parents had used the bracelets to tell them apart when they were younger, though it wasn't long before their personalities made that unnecessary. Still, they kept the charms, swapping out the bracelets as they grew.

On the floor, Telara spotted a brightly colored plastic game piece; a purple cone topped with a tiny spaceship. She hopped down from the dresser, picked it up, and held it in her hand. They played that game many times as kids. She bounced the piece in her palm, amazed it had been left out. Her neat-freak sister would've scooped it up instantly. With a soft sigh, she slipped the piece into her pocket. Another memory only she'd carry.

Since arriving in Sanctuary all those years ago, she and her friends had thought about nothing else. Sanctuary became everything to them; it consumed their thoughts. The Arions, the creatures, and the Shadows ruled by the Shadow Master, Zane. Not to mention the Crims, the battles they fought, and the mystery of who they truly were. But as she stood in her sister's room, her lips curled with quiet sorrow. This was who she truly was, too. And she had taken it for granted. Not once in all the years in Sanctuary had she stopped to think about the life she left behind in Michigan; her family. She looked back at the ticking clock and let out a ragged breath. In just a few more minutes, it'd all be gone, and there was nothing she could do to stop it.

I.Q. had been co-valedictorian alongside Jessa White, who transferred from the Upper Peninsula the year before. While Jessa spoke about looking ahead and thanking the faculty who guided her, I.Q. had chosen a different path. He talked about family and friendships; the things too often taken for granted. He reminded everyone to thank not only those who helped them to succeed, but also the people who had been there through every moment of the journey.

So much had happened this past year; moments they'd remember, even if no one else did. Chad had lost his favorite eccentric uncle, the one who left him an Uno draw-four card in his will. Chad joked about a family dinner where he kept playing draw-fours on his uncle, prompting the old man to swear that he was going to leave him one in his will; and he did. Eccentric or not, he'd kept his word.

They had spent most of their high school years worrying about the battle ahead. And this last year, they'd been trying to hold on to what they were about to lose.

The clock struck six o'clock with a melodic chime. The hands pointed straight up and down, pointing to the twelve and six. Telara's body tensed. Her breathing slowed. Her hands clenched. She didn't know what to expect. She wanted to run to her sister, hold her, wake her up in the hopes that doing so would stop what was about to happen. But she didn't move. She was frozen, as though time itself had paused.

A low humming filled the room. She thought it might be the pool cleaner kicking on. The first summer they had the pool, its cleaning system kept them awake. Their rooms overlooked the backyard pool, and they could climb out onto the roof to dive in; something their mother hated. If it hadn't been an in-ground pool, she would've moved it far from their rooms. After that first summer they had gotten used to the sound, it had even become sort of a lullaby to them. That soft hum, the vibration, would soothe them to sleep.

The pool had hosted so many parties; birthday parties and start-of-summer parties as well as many others. One of those parties they threw, when they were in elementary school, began a tradition of Tiara pushing Chance into the pool. Telara couldn't even remember what Chance had done that first time to earn a dunking, but it became an annual joke. Some said it was the reason he became swim captain; to survive around Tiara.

The hum grew louder, filling the room. Telara glanced at Tiara, torn between wanting her sister to wake up and fearing that she would. Still, Tiara slept. It was as if Telara were the only one who could hear it. The sound intensified until it consumed her hearing. The air thickened. Her vision blurred. And when it cleared, she wasn't alone.

The other Guardians surrounded her, still in their homes, but their visions filled her sister's room.

Cole stood in his kitchen, leaning against the counter, staring ahead, the Firebird's keys clenched in his hand. Tia was curled in the wicker chair in her mother's room, hugging her knees, her tear-streaked face pale. Vanna sat on her living room couch, head leaned back, wrapped in a soft pink throw. I.Q. watched the ticking clock on his kitchen wall. Chad and Chance stood in their game room, identical as ever, both staring at the dartboard clock.

The visions of the others started to swirl around her. Telara turned back to her sleeping sister and moved to grab her. But as her fingers reached out, everything went black.

When she opened her eyes, her squiggly ceiling creatures greeted her, dancing above her bed in the Sanctuary bungalow.

They were back.

Telara sighed and rolled out of bed. She landed lightly on her feet and looked toward the window. Morning light filtered in. Her chest tightened as she imagined her family waking up, without a single memory of her. She turned from the window, blinking back tears.

That's when she saw it, the purple game piece, sitting on

her bedside table. She picked it up and tucked it into her pocket, swallowing hard.

Downstairs, the others were already gathered in the kitchen. No one spoke. They sat around the table, lost in thought, their faces mirrors of her own despair. The table was empty, no one was hungry.

"So, what do we do now?" Telara looked over at Chance but he was staring down at the table looking lost. His question sounded so forlorn.

"I don't know," she admitted. "I don't even know what I'm supposed to feel right now, let alone what to do."

"Train. Train, then die, I guess." Vanna's voice cut through the silence. She lifted her head, eyes sharp. "What else is there? We go out there and train until they send us after this Magine. Until then, we owe them nothing."

Coming from Vanna, those cold words sounded ominous, but each of them understood. One by one, they nodded.

"So," she repeated, her voice hard, "we train."

MANY HOURS LATER, TELARA FOUND HERSELF CROUCHED IN A four-point start position, like a track runner. Her eyes locked onto the course in front of her. Her first obstacle was the river of lava winding through the grassy field; she'd need to cross that. Once she completed that obstacle, she'd have to get through a gauntlet of swinging pendulums tipped with razor-sharp blades. Not only were the ends deadly, but there were blades that jutted out along the rods like thorns on a rose stem. Immediately after the pendulums, there was a climbing wall that towered over twenty feet, studded with obstacles meant to slow her down. She couldn't see what lay beyond the wall, but she had a feeling it wasn't' going to be pleasant.

"Go!" Zeke shouted while some of the other Arions stood by and watched. She wondered how many helped Zeke with this training course. They hadn't seen Ira since coming to Sanctuary, something none of them were upset over. They knew it wasn't Ira's fault, that he didn't make the decision that took them from their families, but that didn't make any of them feel better.

Telara sprang forward, focusing on conjuring invisible planks just ahead of her with each step. Each time she stepped on one, she'd create another, mere inches before her until she cleared the lava and landed on the other side, safe and sound.

The pendulums, however, were a different story. She couldn't go over or around them. She had no choice but to go through them, without becoming shredded cheese. She thought about how Zane taught her to create illusions with her thoughts back in Haven, but she knew they wouldn't help with this.

She slowed down as she studied the swinging blades, her teeth worrying her bottom lip. *There's always a pattern,* she heard I.Q.'s voice in her mind, via their mindlink. *You just need to find it.*

Easy for your analytical mind, she shot back through their mindlink.

She inhaled deeply and advanced, forming a protective barrier around her in case she misread the timing. The first two pendulums swung opposite of each other at a steady pace, so she slid between them cleanly. But the third pendulum came fast and caught her shoulder which knocked her back. She twisted mid-air to avoid the next one, but that left her open as the next blade snagged her arm.

Pain flared. Concern from the others flowed through their link, feeding her own frustration and making it harder to focus. Another pendulum slammed into her barrier, pushing her back. The pressure built, sharp and painful.

With a grunt of frustration, she thrust her barrier outward. The pendulums struck her barrier again and again. She pushed harder; her jaw clenched. Then came the sound of steel tearing and cracking, as her barrier exploded outwards. Pendulums were flung in all directions.

"Whoa!" Arions scrambled out of the way as the shattered blades flew. The Guardians remained still, faces expressionless as they watched the chaos.

Telara looked up just in time to see the climbing wall collapse: a pendulum had embedded itself into its face. She rolled her shoulder and floated upward, gliding over the downed structure and the writhing ivy beneath it. Elma, the wood nymph they met when they first came to Sanctuary, glared at her from the shadows of her trees.

At the end of the course, Telara turned to Zeke, who stood watching with a bemused expression.

"Is that it?" she asked.

He shook his head and laughed. "I want to say that I can't believe you did that, but I'd be lying. How about some rainbow ball and punch at the Cantina?"

Telara shook her head. "Thanks, but we're going back to the bungalow."

Zeke's tone softened. "Everyone was kind of hoping we'd all get together tonight for your first night back. Your friends have missed you."

"Not like we'll be around much longer anyways," Cole muttered as he walked past. Zeke looked taken back.

"See you tomorrow," he added over his shoulder.

2

TELARA STARED up at her ceiling and watched her little squiggly friends playing. The shapes scampered across the ceiling while they leapt over one another in an endless game of chase. Each day, she and the other Guardians had followed the same routine, they woke up, gathered in the kitchen where they'd make their breakfast, then they headed to the training fields to start their training for the day. During that time, they didn't speak verbally to one another. All communication was through their telepathic link. Attempts from others to talk were met with cold silence, swiftly and firmly rebuffed.

They missed the camaraderie they once shared with their friends before the past year changed everything. More than that, they were hurt and weren't willing to risk more pain.

She thought back to that first morning in Sanctuary when they sat at their table staring at untouched plates. No one had an appetite. Their thoughts were full of the families they lost. Tears pricked their eyes, chests tight, and throats closed with grief. They had decided that their only goal would be to take down the Shadow Master's Magine and put an end to their misery. They'd become Sanctuary's weapon against the

Shadow Master, just like those who came before them. The illusion of salvation was gone. There was no magical fix. The unseen leaders already won.

Telara closed her eyes and inhaled deeply, trying to calm the storm inside her. When she opened them again, her ceiling companions were still there, dashing around as if nothing changed.

She tried to suppress the longing that rose in her chest, the persistent hope that when she opened her eyes, Zach would be there. She hadn't seen or spoken to him in over two years. Time hadn't dulled the ache; if anything, it had grown stronger. The last time they spoke was at the Citadel. He had warned her, vaguely as always, about Flint. She wanted answers. This time, she promised herself, if Zach returned, she wouldn't let him leave without them. Thanks to Kyler's glimpse into the past, she had new questions, sharper ones, and she wouldn't accept riddles or half-truths.

All she needed was for Zach to show himself.

She rolled over and closed her eyes when a sound from outside her bedroom door had her turning back over with wide eyes. Jumping out of bed she hurriedly put on her slippers, then rushed out into the hallway looking for the source. No one was there.

"Tia?" she called. "Vanna? Cole? Chad? Chance? I.Q.?"

No response.

She stepped farther into the corridor, her feet carrying her toward the kitchen, the same one where Zach first brought her when they arrived at Sanctuary. She was near the room where they'd once overheard Ira and Lucius talking.

Taking a deep breath, she whispered, body tense, trying to smother the budding hope, "Zach?"

A low chuckle answered her, not Zach's. This voice was deeper, but still familiar.

When she turned the corner, she came face to face with piercing blue eyes. She stumbled back in surprise.

"Zane?" she asked, startled.

Zane raised an eyebrow. "I don't remember there being a Zach last summer." His head tilted as his eyes narrowed slightly. "Although that name does sound familiar to me."

"What are you doing here, Zane?" Her tone turned hard.

His brows rose. "You don't sound very happy to see me."

Telara folded her arms. "I'm not!"

He looked genuinely surprised. "I don't understand why not. I thought you wanted answers."

She let out a bitter laugh. "All looking for answers ever got us was pain and betrayal." Zane's expression shifted. "What? You expect us to keep coming back for more disappointment and let downs? We're done."

"Pam would be disappointed."

"Good," she snapped and turned to walk away. "Maybe then she'll know how we feel."

"You don't think she already does?"

She stopped and took a deep breath. "I don't know. She hasn't been around for me to ask."

"Maybe she cares more about saving your lives than you do."

Telara spun back, jabbing a finger at his chest. "You don't get to lecture me on morality. You're the last person on this whole planet who has the right to lecture anyone on that."

"Fine. No lecture," he said, ignoring her finger. "How about facts then? Or are you content with the lies they've been feeding you?"

"We've been told so many, you'll have to be more specific." She moved away from him, her hands clutching her elbows.

"Okay, specific lies then." He nodded. "How about the ones they've told you about me?"

"Oh please," she scoffed. "What could they possibly lie about when it comes to you?"

"I never meant to harm anyone. Especially your friends."

"Really? What about Gage? What about when you turned him into a Shadow?" she demanded.

"I didn't. I never turned him, or any of the Arions into Shadows," he countered.

She huffed. "Fine. One of your lackeys did. That's still on you."

"She isn't one of my lackeys," Zane muttered. "I guess you could call her my grandmother."

"Your grandmother?" Telara blinked. "The Shadow Master has a grandmother?"

He sighed, lips curling into a wry smile. "Everything you've been told about me and even yourself is a lie. A lie meant to protect others. And yes, I'm just as guilty. I started it."

"So, you admit it!" she said, pointing her finger at him.

"I admit that there are many things I'd done wrong but not what they're accusing me of, come with me and I'll tell you everything." He held out his hand to her.

Telara stared at his hand. "Is that what you told Pam? Is that why she joined you?"

"No. Hard as it may be to believe, she loves her brother. She wanted to be with him, even if she didn't understand his choices. Though… I don't think that's the real reason she's with me." He watched her as he spoke.

Telara's eyes narrowed. "Then what is the reason?"

"She's trying to find a way to save you, all of you, without Sanctuary's constraints."

Telara snorted. "And you're just letting her?"

"I've told her the only way to save you is for you to come to me. But, like you, she doesn't trust easily. She needs to find out for herself. I give her the freedom to do that."

"As long as she does what you want her to do," Telara shot back.

"I give her room and board. I ask for very little in return."

He said it casually, but his eyes tracked her every movement as she paced, keeping her distance.

She stopped and whirled on him. "Like breaking into Sanctuary and stealing Shadows?"

"You had my favorite; I wanted him back."

Silence hung between them before Telara said, her voice tight, "They could've been Arions! They could've been friends!"

"They weren't. Only one was more than a Shadow and I promise that none of you even know him."

"How can you say that?"

"Because he's my friend."

Of all the things she expected him to say, that wasn't one of them. "You turned your own friend into a Shadow?"

"It isn't that simple."

Telara rolled her eyes and mockingly said, "No, you're right, it's not. You're a complicated bag of villain and this conversation is over. We'll train, we'll fight your precious Magine, and we'll die defeating her, so someone else can deal with your riddles."

She turned to leave.

"My Magine?" he queried softly.

She stopped but didn't turn back to look at him.

"I keep hearing about this great evil," he continued, "but somehow, I don't even know who, or what, that is. Funny, isn't it? That I don't even know my own supposed creation?"

She scoffed and turned to face him. "Like I should trust you."

"No, you shouldn't."

She blinked at his honesty.

"You've been lied to from the start. Why would you believe anyone, least of all me? This battle they're preparing you for, it's just a performance."

She raised a brow, but he kept going.

"I have no reason to want you, or your friends, dead."

"You don't?" she asked with skepticism.

He watched her for a long time but said nothing.

Telara gave a silent scoff inside her head; of course, another half-truth.

"I don't think you're ready to know," he finally said.

She scoffed. "You claim to be different from Lucius, but you sound just like him. I should've known better." She waved him off. "You know what? This conversation is over."

"When you're ready to talk, let me know," he said with a sigh.

"Do you even listen when I speak? I said we're done. You're just like the rest. Riddles, secrets, but no answers." She stomped her foot with a grunt. After a moment, she crossed her arms, and looked at him. "But if I were to want to talk to you, exactly how would I even reach you?"

His small smile widened. "It's nice to see you haven't changed."

Her expression darkened. "What?"

"Never mind," he said, cutting her off gently. "Just know that I'll know. And I'll be there."

Just like that, he was gone.

Telara opened her eyes and stared at the ceiling. The shapes were still now, utterly still.

He turned his friend into a shadow?

Telara didn't answer Cole's mental question aloud. She simply gave a small, covert nod as she deflected a volley of electric orbs with her Crim. Her lips curled in bitter disdain.

All the while making himself out to be the victim.

One of the orbs ricocheted off her shield, soaring into the edge of Fable Forest and cracking through a tree trunk. Just another training session and another day pretending they weren't broken.

Their routine hadn't changed: fight, sweat, push past

limits. But underneath it all, none of them felt strong. Their bravado was a mask, stretched too thin.

Back in Haven, Zane had opened their eyes to a terrifying truth; they didn't need their Crims to access their powers. The energy was theirs, buried deep, dormant until drawn out. And now that they knew? They didn't trust it. Not because the power was wrong, but because Zane showed it to them. A traitor. A man they had once trusted. A man most of them had even liked. Vanna had been the only one with reservations about him.

They kept telling themselves that they needed to separate who showed them how to use their powers without their Crims, and them using their powers. They were trying and succeeding mostly, but sometimes the self-doubt would sneak back in.

Vanna twirled her staff, slamming it into the earth. Thick vines burst from the ground, forming a living wall to block a hail of sharp projectiles.

Did he say anything useful? she asked dryly as the vines melted back into the soil.

Telara couldn't stop the snort that escaped. Trent's head turned at the sound, but he said nothing. He had joined Zeke and the rest of the Delta faction, and though they still crossed paths, the warmth was gone. The Guardians gave nothing away, just vague replies and tired smiles.

"We're just here to train," they told anyone who approached them with friendly intentions.

But really? They were too scared to be vulnerable again.

Not really. It's not like we don't know we're being lied to, Telara answered Vanna.

At least we know Pam didn't truly betray us, Tia offered, hovering in the air as winds swirled around her. She dodged the vines that Elma, the wood nymph, sent her way with practiced ease. What once had taken intense focus now felt effortless. Their power had grown, but their hearts had grown distant.

Elma's scream cut through the air as Cole snapped his fingers and her vines erupted in flames. He gave Vanna a look when she glared, but said nothing. Another example of not only how much their powers had grown but also how they were able to use their power without their Crims.

Come on, Telly. Tia's voice was softly spoken via their mental link. *If what Zane told you is true, Pam still wants to help.*

Then she should've stayed. Telara's lips thinned.

Yeah, because we were making such progress. I.Q. launched a wave of electric bolts, vaporizing the last of the incoming projectiles. His expression was impassive as he met Telara's glare. *Tell me I'm wrong.*

Telara exhaled slowly. She didn't have an answer

"Okay, training's done for today."

Trent jogged toward them, casual and hopeful. "You going with us to Czaar's? Gage will be there."

Telara turned away before the guilt could show.

"No, thanks. We need to rest before training tomorrow."

Her voice was flat, distant. Trent's face fell.

"Maybe next time."

She hated how that felt, how much it still hurt to say no to the people they once called friends.

I hate this.

Chance's words rang in their minds, unspoken but shared.

Telara agreed. Every step they took away from their friends felt heavier. Every silent moment, suffocating. But they were too exhausted from betrayals, from trusting and being burned. Cutting themselves off was the only way to stop the bleeding.

Vanna suddenly tensed beside her, and Telara followed her gaze.

Coming from the Theta barracks was Gabe, his grin wide and hopeful as he looked at Vanna.

"Hey!" he called out, waving.

They didn't stop. Didn't look. Just kept walking.

"Hey, guys..." His voice faltered as they passed him in silence.

Their boots scraped against the path as they moved toward their bungalow, backs turned, hearts aching.

But they didn't look back.

3

IRA STOOD STILL beneath the shadowed canopy of Fable Forest; his eyes fixed on the distant shape of the Guardians' bungalow nestled between gnarled trees and moss-covered stones. The forest, alive with gentle rustling and faint glimmers of magic, somehow felt heavier tonight, as if it too bore the weight of what had been lost.

The sound of footsteps crunching through the underbrush broke the quiet. A rustle to his left announced the arrival of Storn, one of the gnomes assigned to quietly monitor the Guardians' well-being. With Lucius no longer available to be there for the Guardians, Ira felt it necessary.

"Ira." The gnome greeted in his usual no-nonsense tone.

"Storn." Ira spoke quietly, as if speaking too loudly might shatter the brittle calm surrounding them. "Anything to report?"

Storn nodded, arms folded behind his back. "They returned to the house a few minutes ago. Straight down to the basement again. They've been training non-stop." He paused before adding, "They barely eat. Speak only to each other, if at all. And sleep? Maybe an hour or two at most. They're running themselves ragged."

Ira exhaled; gaze still fixed on the house. "Maybe they need time. Time to heal, to make sense of everything."

Storn gave a snort, not unkind, but sharp. "Do you truly believe that? Time isn't healing them. It's isolating them. They're not recovering, Ira. They're shutting down."

"I don't have anything to give them," Ira admitted, voice thick with frustration and guilt. "Lucius was the one who kept them tethered. The one they trusted."

"Now, he's gone," Storn said plainly. "Taken by Hades, and without him, they're unraveling."

The silence between them stretched long, broken only by the wind rustling through the trees.

"They're strong," Ira said at last, trying to believe it himself. "They've survived more than most."

"They're not just strong, they're tired," Storn replied. "Wounded. And if no one reaches them soon, they'll burn themselves out before the Magine ever touches them." He turned to leave, his small figure almost vanishing in the thick brush. "We'll keep an eye on them, but they need more than eyes. They need someone to fight for them."

Ira remained still, watching the last sliver of light fade behind the closed door of the Guardians' home. He could almost see them in his mind, shoulders slumped, eyes shadowed, pushing themselves beyond the breaking point. Not because they wanted to win, but because they no longer knew how to stop fighting.

His chest ached with helplessness.

"Lucius," he whispered into the trees. "Wherever you are, we need you. *They* need you. Your Guardians are slipping away."

The wind didn't answer, only stirred the branches above him.

Drawing in a long, steadying breath, Ira turned and disappeared into the woods.

DOWN IN THE REALM OF HADES, THE CELL WAS COLD AND DISMAL. Lucius sat on the floor with his back pressed against the damp stone wall. The only light came from a flickering torch outside his stone prison, its flame struggling against the darkness.

Before him, a vision portal shimmered faintly, revealing Ira vanishing into the forest. "I'm here, old friend," Lucius whispered. "As soon as I can, I'll be back."

Footsteps echoed down the corridor, heavy, measured, and familiar.

"Good luck," came a dry voice.

Lucius didn't have to look to know who it was. Hades stepped into view, his presence as oppressive as the cold. The God of the Underworld stood outside the shimmering containment shield, his pale eyes raking over Lucius with unreadable calm.

Lucius turned his gaze back to the portal, refusing to give Hades the satisfaction.

"You're quiet today," Hades said.

Lucius met his gaze finally, jaw tight. "Trying not to waste breath on someone who prefers the sound of his own lies."

"Still defiant." Hades chuckled humorlessly. "Still clinging to a war that isn't yours."

Lucius rose slowly to his feet. "You mean it isn't mine because it threatens the comfortable empire you've built on blood and silence?"

Hades' expression hardened. "You could've stayed with your friends. Let the cycle play out. Let the Guardians inherit their roles and live in peace."

Lucius took a step forward. "Peace? You mean letting my family be slaughtered again and again, while Larsa tightens her grip on this world? Let her continue in her scheming and ignoring those she hurts in her wake?"

"They aren't your family; they're merely clones. Your family is dead," Hades told him flatly.

Lucius flinched, only barely.

Hades's voice grew sharper. "But your mother lives; why don't you fight for her?"

Lucius's laugh was bitter. "Larsa isn't some misunderstood victim. She's the rot at the center of all of this. She twisted my son against me and used his grief like a blade. You think I'm the danger, but you don't see her for what she is. Or maybe you do, and you don't care."

Lucious started to pace inside the cell, his movements agitated and jerky. "We didn't come here to start a war. We came to take a killer home. To stop her before she could destroy more lives. But instead, your gods turned on us."

"Because you wouldn't stop," Hades growled.

"Because you wouldn't let her go!" Lucius snapped. "The gods murdered innocents to keep her secret safe. You all feared the truth more than justice."

Hades' jaw twitched, the first crack in his mask. "You know nothing of what we've lost."

Lucius turned on him. "Then tell me. Why protect her? Why cage me here while she hunts my friends, while she poisons the minds of the next generation?"

Silence stretched between them, taut and brittle.

"Because you don't understand what it means to love someone despite what they've become," Hades said at last, voice quieter, almost mournful. "Because you haven't had to watch your child turn into something monstrous...and still believe there's something left to save."

Lucius stared at him, uncertain now. "Are you talking about Zane?" How would Hades know about Zane? He never told him. Never told anyone what Larsa did to his son, how she'd turn Zane's love into a weapon for her to use.

"You've lost your mind," he muttered, more to himself than Hades.

"I haven't," Hades said quietly. "But I have lost time. Time I can't get back. And now, I'm trying to protect what's left. If that means keeping you locked away, then so be it."

Lucius exhaled slowly, voice rough. "You're protecting the wrong person."

When Hades didn't answer him, Lucius resumed pacing, the questions boiling inside him. "Why her? The gods killed entire bloodlines without blinking. What made this one different? Why would it matter if the world knew what you'd done?"

"We didn't kill them!" Hades shouted at him; the whole cavern shook with his anger.

Lucius stared, his heated expression cooled. His eyes narrowed on Hades while his mouth became a hard line. "Then who did?"

Hades straightened, the flames in his eyes receded. His hands clenched into fists as he pressed his lips together tightly. "It doesn't matter." His words were spoken in a harsh tone. Lucius opened his mouth to speak but Hades cut him off. "Besides, they weren't innocents! They were the children of the Paladins," Hades practically sneered.

"The Paladins did nothing to you." Lucius countered. "They came for justice, that's all. They came to stop a killer."

"They came to take my daughter from me!" Hades shouted back at him.

Lucius's breath caught as his thoughts stumbled. "Your daughter is Larsa?"

Hades said nothing.

Lucius turned back to the vision portal. The Guardians were there, his Guardians, huddled in separate rooms, weary and withdrawn. Still fighting. Still loyal.

"You want me to forget what she's done," Lucius said. "But I won't. Because if I do, she wins. And she'll keep winning. Until someone stops her."

"I just want her to be happy," Hades whispered.

"And I just want her to pay," Lucius snapped.

Neither man spoke after that. The silence was worse than shouting.

Finally, Hades stepped back into the shadows, his voice cold again. "Then I suppose we're enemies."

Lucius didn't flinch. "We always were."

IRA WATCHED THE GUARDIANS AS THEY TRAINED WITH MEMBERS of both the Alpha and Delta factions, his fingers laced loosely in front of him and expression unreadable. Their movements were clean, efficient, and brutal. Once, their strength had come from passion, the need to protect. Now, it was precision born from pain. They fought like they had nothing left to lose. He knew that was how they felt. He couldn't blame them, but this was self-destructive. He wanted to think of them as only soldiers without a story. Now, thanks to Lucius, these kids managed to worm their way into all the hearts of Sanctuary, including his. He didn't want this and now Lucius wasn't even here to yell at about it.

"This isn't training," he muttered. "It's a war rehearsal."

Behind him, Storn shifted uncomfortably. "They haven't spoken to anyone. They eat the bare minimum, sleep even less."

Ira nodded slowly, his jaw clenched. "I've spoken with the Leaders."

Storn frowned. "And?"

"They say the leniency Lucius was granted is over. From here on, they want full compliance."

Storn looked alarmed. "Then what do we do?"

Ira didn't answer immediately. He just stared as Telara knocked her opponent flat with a single, ruthless strike. Then he said, "We do nothing."

The gnome blinked. "What?"

"I think the Guardians need a change of scenery," Ira mused.

Storn raised a brow. "And how do we arrange that when they're technically forbidden to leave Sanctuary?"

Ira allowed a small, knowing smile. "The Leaders said I can't let them leave Sanctuary. They didn't say anything about someone requesting them."

Storn's eyes widened. "You're thinking of Jerry."

Ira nodded. "Didn't he ask for help recently with shoring up Arcadia's defenses?"

"Yes, but he wanted Arions," Storn countered.

"Well, he's getting Guardians instead. Provided they keep up their training."

Storn grinned. "You've definitely been around Lucius too long."

"You have no idea," Ira murmured. "Let Jerry know. I'll speak to the Guardians myself."

But even as Storn hurried off, Ira's thoughts were already turning to someone else. Someone whose influence could shift the balance, if she could be convinced.

Night had long since fallen since Ira's conversation with Storn. Ira slipped into the lower levels of Sanctuary, behind a warded archway few dared to approach. The ward placed on this archway kept out unwanted visitors.

Ira moved past the archway into the inner chamber where Gwin waited for him. She stood before the glowing runes that kept this place secret from all, even Lucius. Gwin turned to smile at him. In her hand, she carried a staff made from the stem of a colossal dandelion, the top crowned with radiant white tufts that shimmered like stardust, constantly releasing tiny glowing seeds that floated gently in the air around her.

Her hair cascaded around her in white ringlets, glowing faintly like moonlight on snow. The curls spilled from beneath a wreath of vibrant green leaves. She wore a white, filmy top that clung lightly to her form like morning mist on petals. Coiling green vines wrapped around her arms; they seemed to be living and pulsing with subtle magic. She wore a belt of green leaves around her waist, that rested atop a soft, sheer white skirt that draped around her legs like spun gossamer.

On her feet, she wore white high-heeled boots, laced with green vines that spiraled up her calves like growing ivy. She radiated pure earth energy; her and Vanna would complement one another, but Gwin had no desire to interact with the Guardians.

"You're late," Gwin told him, standing with her staff held horizontally in front of her. One hand gripped it firmly, while the other rested across her wrist, steadying it.

Ira narrowed his eyes on her, but her stance and stare never wavered. "You knew I was coming? How? I didn't even know that I'd come to you."

"I always know when you need me."

Ira leveled her with a stare, but she remained unfazed, standing patiently as she waited for him to speak. He drew in a deep breath before finally breaking the silence. "They're unraveling."

"We've noticed."

Ira's face went slack with the shock of her words. "You've noticed?" He asked her, his tone showing his disbelief. She said nothing but nodded at his words, he swallowed hard, trying to tamp down the anger that built at her coldly rationally spoken words. "How can you be so stoic about this? We're talking about our- "

"I know exactly what we're talking about." Gwin told him sharply. "I also haven't forgotten what's at stake if we fail, have you?"

"Of course not." Ira breathed in deeply, his hand moving to rake his fingers through his hair in agitation.

"We don't get a second chance," Gwin told him, her voice softening as she moved closer to him. She placed a placating hand on his shoulder, a small smile on her face when he looked over at her. "We can't let our feelings get in the way of what has to be done, no matter how much it hurts, the end game is bigger than any of us."

"I can't watch them self-destruct, not when I can do something about it." Ira told her, moving away from her and shaking off her hand.

"You haven't shown any distaste for the plan before," Gwin pointed out to him.

He turned back to her. "Before, they had Lucius. Now, he's gone and we don't know when he'll be back."

"Or if," Gwin said.

"You think he's dead?"

"I think time is running out either way."

The silence hung between them at her words, Ira looked perplexed as he pondered her words while she stood there watching him. Finally, she said, "you want to buy them time?"

Ira paused before he responded, "Yes."

"Then give them purpose. Not just more drills. Something real. Something they can grasp."

"Training is all they'll accept right now."

"They don't need training," she said sharply. "They need grounding. They need to feel needed, not just used." She stepped past him, her town lowering. "Arcadia. Jerry has been requesting help. Send them there."

Ira stared at her for a moment before responding. "You already knew I'd suggest that," he accused her.

Her lips curled into a smile, "I suggested it, you just haven't realized it yet."

Ira frowned at her before a grin broke out, "Careful Gwin, your feelings are starting to show."

She raised a petite brow at him, "Don't mistake my

actions. I believe that sending them there is necessary for them to do what they have to."

"The others?" Ira asked her.

"They will see it the same way as me. The Guardians taking this assignment will keep them occupied, focused, and away from Sanctuary's politics. If it fails, no one important will notice. If it succeeds, maybe they will begin to remember who they truly are."

"What are the others expecting from this?" Ira asked her.

"Balance." At his frown she reminded him, "We aren't the only ones with secrets, you have your own. Not even Lucius figured it out."

Ira didn't care for that answer, but he didn't challenge it.

"I'll speak to them tomorrow," he finally said.

"Good. You've been too soft with them." She raised a brow. "Don't be soft now."

"I'm not Lucius," he said.

"No," she agreed. "But someone has to lead them until he returns, or until they break."

With that she turned and vanished into the shadows behind the ancient archway, leaving Ira alone in the stillness.

Ira stood there for a long moment, then whispered into the silence, "Come back soon, Lucius. They need you; I can't do what you can do for them."

4

THE TRAINING HALL was alive with movement, grunts of exertion, fists hammering into sandbags, and the occasional bursts of elemental energy against the scorched walls. Sweat glistened on the Guardian's brows, but none of them stopped.

They hadn't stopped for weeks.

Telara floated a few feet above the ground on one of her invisible platforms, poised to launch Zeke across the room when a familiar voice cut through the din.

"Enough training for today."

She turned to see Gage leaning against the doorframe, arms crossed casually. This was only the third time they'd seen him since returning to Sanctuary.

She frowned. "It isn't even evening yet."

"You've done nothing but train since you've been back. Time to take a break. Silest is making a feast for everyone, she wanted me to make sure to tell you guys that she missed seeing you all." He told them.

"We're not here to socialize," Telara said flatly, still hovering. "We're here to train."

"Yes, you will," came a deeper voice. "But not here."

They all turned. Ira stood just inside the training hall, arms loosely crossed in front of him, expression unreadable.

"What do you mean?" Telara asked, crossing her arms tightly.

"The leaders aren't satisfied with your attitude," Ira said. His words hit like a slap, but Telara didn't flinch.

"So?" she fired back. "All they care about is that we march to our deaths against the Magine, our attitudes won't change that."

"If they don't like it, then they can find someone else to die for them," she added bitterly.

"I understand your aggravation," Ira said.

"Do you?" Telara interrupted him. "Our lives just got erased so that we can go on a suicide mission."

"Fighting those who were once our friends," Cole added, his usual grin nowhere to be found.

Tia grimaced, "let's not forget being sent into the Shadow Master's domain. Remember the Citadel? Haven?"

"You really think I wanted any of that to happen to you?" Ira glared at them. "I was against you growing up with parents to get attached to only to have them yanked away from you. I didn't want you exposed to anyone outside of Sanctuary knowing the heartache that could be brought to you with your short existence." Ira took a deep breath. "Yeah, the Guardians were treated well above all the others here at Sanctuary; our ancestors felt that they deserved something for giving up their lives as they were destined to do. I tried to follow those rules." Ira told them.

"We deserve to live!" Vanna said, her voice trembling.

Ira breathed in deeply as his gaze softened, remorse shining in his eyes. "Yes, you do."

A heavy silence fell, until Chance finally asked, "Where are we going?"

"We've got a compound in Florida," Ira replied. "Not a battlefield, more like a research facility of sorts. Lucius' friend, Jerry, runs it. He needs help securing their defenses, too many Shadow attacks have thinned their resources. Could help in the fight against the Magine. You'll still train. Just... somewhere new."

"Research facility of sorts?" I.Q. frowned. "What does that mean?"

Ira hesitated, his jaw tightening. "It's... complicated. You'll see."

"And if we refuse?" Telara asked, her arms still crossed while she stood on her platform. She fought the temptation to knock Ira off his feet, she knew it'd cause them nothing but more problems if she did. She hated this feeling of not having any control over her life. Whoever these leaders were, she hoped their beds were full of Legos at night. Chance cringed at her thought but stayed silent while they waited to see what Ira would say.

"I can't force you," Ira said. "Honestly? I don't even know if sending you is the right call. This feels like something Lucius would've done. Not me."

He turned slightly. "I'll tell the Leaders you're not interested. Maybe they'll come up with another plan." As he started to walk away, the Guardians exchanged glances.

Gage watched the exchange but didn't say anything as the Guardians looked at each other.

Lucius has a best friend? Vanna asked silently.

Do you think he knew who Lucius really was? I.Q. mused while attempting to look as if they weren't discussing things via their internal link.

I don't know about you guys, but I'm getting kind of bored here. Some new scenery might not be a bad thing. Tia suggested, her fingers creating mini tornados in the air around her to cloak their mind-speak.

Telara sighed, lowering her platform. "Fine, we'll go."

Ira stopped and turned, one brow raised. "Are you sure?

Wouldn't you rather just stay here and find creative ways to defy the Leaders?"

She studied him. There was something in his tone, a sharpness, a flickering of something less jaded. Maybe hope. Maybe guilt. She wasn't sure, but wasn't going to spend too much time thinking about it.

"We're going." She told him, her chin held high. "Just let us pack, won't take us long, not like we have much."

She walked off without another word, the others following her towards their bungalow.

Gage moved closer to Ira watching them walk away. "So… the Leaders really want them to go to Florida?" He asked.

Ira arched a brow. "Did I say that?"

Gage chuckled. "You sly dog."

"I don't know what you're talking about." Ira replied, voice dry. Then, he spoke more softly. "Can you handle their travel?"

"Yeah, I can get that handled." Gage assured him.

"Thank you." Ira nodded before walking away.

"Hey!" Gage stopped Ira who turned to look at him. "Any news on Lucius?"

Ira paused and after a long silence, he gave a silent shake of his head and continued walking. The weight of unspoken things following him like a shadow.

"What? No special transportation?" Cole frowned as they entered the porter room in the Gamma quarters. Gage turned to greet them when they entered, his brow furrowed at Cole's question.

"Special transportation?" Gage queried.

"Yeah," Chad jumped in. "Portals hidden in the forest. That railcar that vanishes underground. Even that floating glass bubble. Y'know, something with flair."

Footsteps echoed… measured and unhurried. Claw

strolled in, leather jacket creaking, one hand buried in his pocket and boots striking the floor like punctuation. "Since the incident wi' Haven, all that's been shut down," he spoke. "Tae much risk. Now, everythin' runs through this porter. Only way in and out."

"Why?" I.Q. asked, brows drawing together.

"Because of Zane," boomed Tobias as he entered, voice deep and final. "They allowed him to keep Haven unconnected so no one could visit without him knowing."

"And no one would find out that he was the Shadow Master." Telara added, her voice cold, a bitter edge undercutting her calm.

The Arions around them nodded in grim agreement.

"Jerry knows you guys are coming, " Gage said, shifting the mood. "He will make sure that you guys are able to keep up your training while there."

As the porter tech moved silently around them, preparing the platform for their departure, tension flickered among the group.

Before anyone could ask more, the tech turned to them. "Everything's ready. Time to go," he briskly told them, moving from the platform to the control panel.

One by one, the Guardians stepped forward. The opaque glasses felt heavier than expected as they slid them on. Light shimmered beneath their feet. Soft at first, then impossibly bright, until it devoured the room, the porter and the very air around them.

When the light faded, Sanctuary was gone.

Instead, they stood in a plain room that looked disappointingly mundane. Stacked chairs, circular brown tables and bland walls

"Welcome to Arcadia."

They turned to find a brown-haired girl watching them, hip cocked, her shirt emblazoned with a bunny riding a horse. Jeans, worn sneakers, and the kind of gaze that said she'd seen more than she let on. Four kids stood at her side; each quiet, alert, and too young to be this serious.

"Arcadia?" I.Q. looked around them at the room with a frown. "This doesn't look like some utopian paradise to me."

"Yeah, well, to the outside world, this is considered a retirement community in Florida in the middle of a gulf course called the Hills. So, we have to keep up the appearance. To those that truly matter, they know this is Arcadia." The girl shot back.

"I didn't mean to offend." I.Q. attempted to placate her but she just held up her hand.

"Please, I'm not that thin-skinned. Just stating a fact." The girl told them dismissively. "I'm Kasey and I lead the Vanguards."

"The Vanguards?" Cole frowned.

"Yep." She jerked a thumb over her shoulder. "We keep Arcadia running while our grandparents handle lab work and field ops."

She held out her hand to them, Telara stayed back as Vanna moved forward to shake the hand.

"This is Jacob, my second in command." Kasey said, indicating a sandy-haired boy with curious eyes and a quiet energy.

"Allison and Carter are brother and sister. They like to tinker and their creations have been very beneficial to Arcadia." The blond pair gave brief nods, their matching attire smudged with faint grease stains.

The smallest girl whispered in Kasey's ear, her long dark curls swaying with her movement. She wore a flowered sundress and white sandals. Kasey nodded to her. "You're right, Lillie. Jerry is waiting for us." She turned towards the Guardians. "We should be going."

"Jerry runs this place, right?" Tia asked as they exited into the sunlit afternoon.

"Yeah, he runs the place and what he wants with you, he

hasn't informed us." It was Kasey who answered. "We just know that we were to pick you up and take you to him. He said something about coming up with training sessions for you." She shrugged. "We're just the welcome crew."

"Training sessions?" Telara gave a wry expression. "What kind of training prepares you to die?"

Silence fell, the question echoing louder than intended. The younger kids stared, expressions unreadable.

"Telara." Vanna said softly, warning.

Telara shrugged. "It's the truth, why sugarcoat it?"

"Let's just go see Jerry." Tia suggested and a look of relief crossed the kid's faces.

It isn't their fault, Telara. Vanna reprimanded Telara via the mind link, but Telara followed the kids and said nothing.

Outside, the sun was sharp and golden, while the air was humid. A row of golf carts stood waiting, each custom painted and tricked out with modifications. One gleamed blue with yellow flames, another was bright red with a canopy and extra seating, while a third looked like an orange jeep.

Kasey hopped into the red cart while the others climbed into the other two. She turned to look at them. "You coming or would you rather walk?"

The Guardians shared a look, half amusement, half resignation, before they climbed aboard.

As they rolled through Arcadia, the Guardians took it in. A sea of mobile homes arranged like a suburban maze. Neatly trimmed lawns, ceramic gnomes, and plastic flamingos. Nothing magical, nor arcane that they could see.

No crystal towers, no swirling energy fields, and no ethereal creatures lurking in plain sight. Just quiet.

Suddenly Chad jerked around and attempted to climb over the seat and almost landed in Vanna's lap. Vanna glared at him.

"What is wrong with you?" She shoved him.

"Did you see that?" Chad jerked his head back and forth looking around them.

"What?" Vanna groused and shoved him back towards his seat but he was still craning his neck to look at what he was trying to find.

"A crocodile!" Chad spun around to look behind them. "I swear I saw it!"

"Why don't you go pet it?" Vanna muttered.

"I doubt you saw a crocodile." Cole said laughing. "They don't just hang around here."

"You have to go down a lot further to find crocodiles." Kasey agreed, maneuvering through a roundabout. She gave a casual wave to an elderly couple walking a fluffy white poodle.

"See? I told you." Cole grinned, triumphant.

"What you probably saw was an alligator." Kasey added, glancing back.

Cole's grin faltered. "Wait.. what?"

"It's probably Henry," Carter told them from the top of the cart.

"Henry?" Telara looked at Tia, alarmed.

"You'll see," Allison told them with a grin.

The cart pulled up to a yellow-sided double-wide with an enclosed lanai. A carport shaded a green golf cart rigged with oversized tires. It looked completely and utterly ordinary.

But as the Guardians stepped out, unease prickled their skin. Something about Arcadia whispered of secrets hidden in plain sight, and their journey, it seemed, was only just beginning.

5

THE GUARDIANS APPROACHED the house cautiously, their footsteps slowing as a tall figure emerged from the doorway.

The man stood easily over six feet, lean and straight-backed, dressed in slacks and a button-up shirt. Looking down they saw he wore cowboy boots, something that looked so out of place in the Florida sun. A crown of silver ringed his otherwise bald head, and a warm, knowing smile lit his face. He radiated calm, but it only seemed to make the Guardians more on edge.

Cole blinked up at him, momentarily forgetting his wariness. "You're… really tall," he breathed.

The man laughed, extending his hand with ease. "Hello, I'm Jerry."

As he spoke, a petite woman stepped out from behind him. Her silver hair curled softly around her kind face, and her presence beside Jerry somehow deepened the sense that this place, and the people, were too normal. Almost deliberately so.

"And this," Jerry added with quiet affection, "is my better half, Lin."

She offered a gentle smile, but the Guardians didn't return

it right away. Their gazes flickered to one another, silent questions passing between them.

Telara finally stepped forward and took his hand, firm and guarded. "Hi, I'm Telara."

"I know," Jerry replied with a cryptic grin. "I've heard a great deal about each of you." He gestured toward the open door. "Please, come in."

Telara hesitated, then nodded, leading the others inside. They crossed into the screened lanai several feet before they froze.

"What the-" Chance stumbled back, nearly tripping over his own feet. "Is that...?!" He stuttered out pointing downwards.

All eyes snapped to the floor. Sprawled in the shade of a wicker loveseat, eyes half-lidded in the heat, was a massive alligator. Its dark, prehistoric body looked entirely out of place on the pastel tiles. Its tail flicked once. Slowly.

Vanna instinctively pressed herself against the nearest wall. "Is that real?" she hissed.

"That," Jerry said, utterly unbothered, "is Henry."

Tia looked nervously down at Henry. "He sure has a lot of teeth."

Jerry chuckled. "He's harmless. A big ol' pussycat."

Cole peeked out from behind Vanna. "He looks like he eats cats." Vanna nodded in agreement as she watched Henry, who seemed unbothered by their presence.

Jerry turned his gaze to Vanna, his expression suddenly thoughtful. "Aren't you the Guardian of nature?"

Vanna's brow furrowed. "What does that have to do with anything?"

Jerry looked down at her. "Alligators are part of nature. Just like your squirrels and bunnies."

"Squirrels and bunnies don't look as menacing," she countered, arms folding.

"Very true," he agreed calmly. "But has Henry given you any reason to feel threatened?"

"He's a gator!" Cole burst out, still glued to the wall.

Vanna, breathing deeply, glanced at Henry again. "He hasn't done anything… yet."

"But he could," Tia pointed out, still inching toward the doorway.

"But he isn't doing anything to us," Vanna said as she moved forward.

"Vanna!" Telara gasped. She tensed, the others mirroring her actions. Their shoulders tight, knees slightly bent, and their hands in front of them, preparing for whatever came next.

Henry watched Vanna with those cold, ancient eyes, unmoving. Then, slowly, she crouched before him and extended a hand.

"Don't," Chance whispered. "Don't pet the gator… it's not a cat, Van."

Vanna touched his snout. The alligator blinked once at her. Then, to their collective horror, Henry nuzzled her hand like a contended dog.

The Guardians stared in amazement.

"He's friendly," Vanna said with a small, amazed smile, brushing her hand along the rough scales.

"We'll take your word for it," Chance muttered, not moving from his post near the doorframe.

Jerry just laughed, his voice like worn leather and firelight. "Come on in. Dinner's just about ready. We can get you all settled into your rooms before dinner."

Still stunned, they filed inside, keeping a wary eye on Henry, who watched them pass by with a slow blink and what looked suspiciously like a reptilian grin. Only Vanna dared to be close to Henry, casting him one last glance before she stepped through the door and into the main part of the house.

Pam looked up from the creaky porch, eyeing her brother who stood above her. She sat on one of the broken steps leading to the porch of the dilapidated house that Zane, the Shadow Master, used as a base. It looked like something from a horror film, cracked shutters, sagging steps, and warped wood barely holding together. Yet inside, it housed Zane's fighters, deserters from Sanctuary and loyal Shadows. Somehow, it still stood.

"Is there somewhere else I should be?" She replied coolly.

Flint shrugged, "I don't know, I'm not sure where you should be."

Pam frowned and followed his gaze out toward the desolate landscape. She didn't know where they were, nothing of their surroundings even hinted at their location. When she asked Zane, he just said that Sanctuary wasn't the only one able to hide their location. After a moment of silence, she asked, "Do you have something to say?"

He breathed in deeply before he looked back down at her. "Why are you here, sis?" He asked her.

Pam's eyes widened at his words. "You wanted me here and now that I'm here, you ask why I'm here?"

He nodded. "Yeah. I wanted you here, but only if you wanted to be here." He chuckled lightly as she raised a skeptical brow at his words. "Sis, I've been waiting for you to see that the status quo of Sanctuary was wrong. That you were being lied to. I thought when you made friends with the Guardians and realized that they didn't have to die, you'd finally understand that everything we've been told was a lie."

"I have realized that." She frowned at him. "That's the reason I'm here."

"Yeah, you're here but you don't talk with anyone here but me and Zane. We have friends here, you know. Friends who've been lied to and friends who've looked up to you. They feel as if you're angry at them."

"Flint, I'm not here to mother the Arions who've joined because they're mad and decided to run away."

His eyes widened and he stepped back slightly. "Isn't that the pot calling the kettle black, little sister?"

Pam rose from her seat, meeting her brother's gaze. "I'm not running," she said.

"Really?"

She shook her head. "Nope, I'm here to try to save my friends. Both you and Zane promised me that I could save them if I joined with you guys. You told me that I wouldn't find the answer within the walls of Sanctuary. Did you guys lie to me to get your way? Because since I've been here, Zane has sent me on small little missions that have nothing to do with saving them and you're trying to talk to me about becoming a leader of traitors. That's not what I came here for."

She didn't raise her voice, but her words were spoken with purpose. Her eyes locked onto his and her stance never softened.

Flint watched his sister without saying anything for a few moments. His face screwed up into a thoughtful expression before it softened and his lips curled up into a smile. "That's the Pammy I remember. Refusing to follow with blind faith, asking questions and demanding answers at the same time."

Pam folded her arms. "When have I ever followed with blind faith?"

"Ira," Flint said without hesitation. "You trust him completely."

"That's not fair, if not for Ira, I wouldn't have been Alpha leader." She told him. "He's always believed in me."

"That doesn't mean you owe him blind loyalty. Ira enforced the same lies you're now fighting against," he countered.

"Whose lies did he spread and enforce?" Pam asked him. "You can't bring me here, then keep me in the dark. That's no better than what you're accusing Sanctuary of doing." She accentuated her words with a finger poke to his chest in her ire.

"Your sister has a right to hear the truth."

They turned to see Zane leaning against one of the porch's sagging posts, watching them with amused detachment.

Pam's eyes narrowed at him. "You're no better. You promised me that you'd help me save the Guardians, you said that you wanted to save them but yet, you've done nothing either."

"I won't explain myself to you. I don't explain myself to anyone." He raised a hand when Pam opened her mouth, her eyes blazing at him. "But I'll tell you that I've been working on that solution as well. I just wasn't ready to let you in on my plans."

"And you are now?" She asked, arms folded tightly.

"Maybe some of them."

She frowned at him. "And this makes you different, how? You're still keeping things from me."

"And yet, I've told you more than anyone at Sanctuary. Including your friend Ira, who I don't blame as much as Lucius." She frowned at his words, so he continued. "I believe that Ira was being kept in the dark as well. Although, I'm sure his reason for not standing up to anyone is that he likes his position of power. A power that's truly not even his."

"You want to explain that to me?"

Zane watched her silently, leaning back against one of the withered posts on the porch. "Have you ever met the Leaders who run Sanctuary?" He asked her.

She shook her head. "No, only Lucius and Ira speak with them."

"Ira may have spoken with them, but I highly doubt that he's laid eyes on them," Zane told her.

"How do you speak with someone without seeing them?" Pam frowned looking back and forth between her brother and Zane.

"The Leaders are very secretive about their identities, they don't like anyone knowing who they are." He told her. "That way, they can operate from the shadows, quietly executing their plans without drawing attention."

Pam arched a brow. "Operating from the shadows. That's rich coming from you."

Zane smirked. "Makes you wonder who the real bad guys are, doesn't it?"

Pam said nothing, her jaw tight.

Zane pushed off the post and walked closer. "Good guys don't hide behind anonymity. If they were truly noble, they'd lead from the front, not manipulate from the back."

Both of Pam's brows arched. "You don't have much room to talk when it comes to hiding behind anonymity."

Zane gave her a grin. "True, but then again, I've never claimed to be a good guy."

Pam nodded in acknowledgement after a moment. "So, what's the plan?" she asked, still skeptical.

"We're going to find out who they are, then we're going to confront them, but I can't do that without any help. They make sure they're very well protected, something I think should end." Lucius told her.

"Maybe they have a reason for that," Pam suggested.

"Really?" Zane raised a brow at her. "You truly think that?" he asked.

"You kept your identity secret while you ran Haven," Pam threw back at him.

Instead of anger, Zane laughed. "This is why I wanted you on my side, I need someone who won't just agree with everything. I want someone who isn't going to simply follow orders to be following orders."

"I have a mind of my own and I use it," Pam told him

simply. "I'm still not convinced of your theory regarding the Leaders, though."

"What if the Leaders are the reason the Guardians are being sent to die?" he challenged.

Pam frowned at Zane's question. "Funny, last I knew it was your Magine that was responsible for that."

Zane's expression sobered. "A Magine I didn't create. One I know nothing about. And I never wanted the Guardians to die. I want one thing, my family back. Just like you'd do anything to save your friends, I'd do anything to get mine back."

"So, what kind of help are you wanting from me?" Pam tilted her head and watched Zane.

"I'm not asking you to convince your friends to follow me. That wasn't part of our deal," Zane said.

She nodded, wary. "Good. Because I won't."

"We already have the contacts we need in Sanctuary," Zane added.

Pam spun to glare at Flint with an accusing glare. "You didn't. Flint, they're your friends."

Her brother shifted his weight and folded his arms with a huff. "That is why I reached out to them, they're my friends and I want them to have the full story. They should be able to make their own decisions."

Pam snorted. "You call that fair?"

Flint shrugged. "You make your own mind up, Pammy, just like they do." He looked at Zane, then back at Pam. "I have to meet up with a friend, I'll see you tonight."

Pam opened her mouth to give Flint a piece of her mind but Zane placed a hand on her shoulder. "Let your brother go, he has his way of helping his friends and you have yours."

She turned to glare at him. "His way puts his friends in morally gray territory, mine is to help my friends."

Zane smirked, a twinkle in his eye. "Then start saving them."

6

THE HOUSE DIDN'T LOOK like much from the outside, just another mobile home nestled in the middle of the retirement community the outside world believed it to be. The door from the lanai closed behind them as they followed Jerry inside. When Jerry opened a side door and led them down some stairs, everything changed.

They followed Jerry into what they thought was just a basement. Instead, they found a sprawling underground hallway lit with soft, glowing sconces and lined with smooth, metallic walls that felt too clean, too modern for the outside world above.

"This is the lower level," Jerry explained. "Every home in Arcadia is connected through here, including Lumenhall, where you first arrived. Most assume it's only a community center, but it's a little more... advanced than that. You'll see soon enough."

Telara's eyes narrowed at his words, though she said nothing. Chance muttered under his breath, "And we thought this place might be a bit more normal."

I didn't. Cole snorted via their mind link. *Not sure we'd even know normal if it hit us in the face.*

"This way," Jerry said, leading them down a corridor that stretched far beyond what should have been possible, given the mobile home's footprint. They listened as Jerry pointed out and named the rooms as they passed. The hallway branched in several directions, a maze of living quarters, common areas, and more doors than any of them could count.

As they walked, faint noises drifted from around the corner. They heard laughter, raised voices and the soft hum of conversation. Jerry paused in front of a set of doors and turned to them. "Your bags are already in your rooms. Pick any that isn't marked. You'll find them well-stocked and comfortable. We don't stand on ceremony around here."

Before they could respond, a shout came from down the hall.

"What? You don't think I'm capable of carrying my own tray because I'm handicapped?"

The Guardians froze and looked at Jerry who was smiling as if he hadn't heard anything. "I will send someone for you when dinner is ready." He smiled and moved past them.

They frowned as they watched him continue walking down the hallway.

"That's not what I meant, Dee," a flustered male voice responded and pulled their attention back to the set of doors that were slightly opened.

"Then it must be because I'm a female, right?" The voice, Dee, grew sharper.

They edged toward the source of the noise and peeked into what Jerry called the Social Room. It was a wide, cozy lounge where several residents had gathered. A stocky guy with light wavy hair stood awkwardly in front of a girl in a wheelchair. Her dark curls bounced as she argued, her tray wobbling dangerously on her lap.

If she keeps moving her body in that manner, she's going to knock that tray off her lap. Chance spoke internally to them as they watched the scene in front of them. It felt like they were watching a train wreck, unable to look away.

You wanna tell her that? his brother shot back.

Chance didn't respond, but he did give an empathetic shake of his head. No one asked Cole but he gave a shake as well, wanting to make sure they knew his position on it.

Not it, Tia interjected as well with a grin.

No one asked you, Cole grumbled through their link.

"Sarah has more on her plate than I do, did you offer to carry hers for her? Or how about Luanne?" Dee started to move her wheelchair closer to Gary who was doing his best to put himself away from her and the situation. His hands out in front of him as if ready to ward off an attack. "Oh wait, what about Jeffery?" she continued.

She isn't going to let this go. Vanna gave a small shake of her head.

"Never mind," Gary mumbled and quickly leapt over a nearby garbage receptacle to avoid Dee, who still glared at him. Gary saw them and relief washed over his face as he moved towards them." You must be the Guardians," he said quickly. "Jerry told me you'd be arriving, I can show you to your rooms."

They nodded, and he hurried forward.

Probably wanting to put a lot of distance between him and Dee. The others gave discreet nods to Chad's silently spoken words.

"You always have problems with her?" Cole asked him, once they were out of earshot.

Gary exhaled. "She's…passionate."

"That's one word for it." Telara snorted.

"She lost the use of her legs in a Shadow incident," Gary continued, and Telara groaned inwardly.

Way to go, T. Telara glared at Cole, who just smirked, most likely enjoying the fact that for once, he wasn't the one putting their foot in their mouth.

"She wasn't pleasant before that happened," Gary continued, unaware of their silent conversation. "But now she's got a chip the size of a mountain."

"She does have a point, though," Vanna said as she brushed her fingers along the wall.

Gary sighed. "Not another one."

Vanna stopped in her tracks. "Excuse me?"

"Nothing," he said hastily. "This room's yours," he added, opening the nearest door. "The rest are up for grabs. Just don't pick one with a nameplate." Without waiting for more questions, Gary darted away, clearly eager to avoid further conflict.

"Probably afraid she'll chase him down the hallway," Cole muttered, ducking into a room without a nameplate on the door.

"Gary!" Telara called after him.

He turned around reluctantly. "Yeah?"

"Do you know when we'll start our training?"

Gary frowned and lifted his shoulders in confusion. "That's something you'll have to take up with Jerry. All I was told was that Sanctuary was sending you guys instead of one of the Factions. Sorry." He disappeared before she could reply.

The rooms they each chose were surprisingly spacious. Each with a soft bed, a closet and an en suite bathroom. Their bags were already inside, just as Jerry had promised. Still, Telara frowned. *How did they know which room we'd pick?* She questioned via their mind link.

Nothing magical about this place on the outside, but definitely on the inside, Tia spoke, and everyone sent agreement vibes.

A LIGHT TAP ON THEIR DOORS ANNOUNCED DINNER, WHEN THEY opened their doors they saw an elderly lady who only stood about three feet tall. She stood there hunched over, her hands gripped a cane that looked as if it was carved from gnarled, ancient wood, its surface weathered with knots and grooves. Her wild white hair jutting out in every direction like a halo of static.

She might be small and frail, but I get a feeling we shouldn't underestimate her, I.Q. spoke and the others nodded in agreement.

"Follow me, children," she told them as she turned and started walking down the hallway. "And just remember, talking about someone, even though they can't hear, is still considered rude." Her raspy voice didn't hold any censure; it actually sounded amused.

"What's your name?" Vanna asked as they followed her.

"You can call me Ruby," she told them.

"I'm sorry, Ruby, we didn't mean to offend you," Vanna told her, her voice full of regret.

Ruby lifted her shoulders. "It takes more than some silently spoken words to offend me. Although there are some pansy babies around here that might cry about it, and they cry so loud that even level-headed baldies have to say something." She rolled her eyes and looked up at them and tapped her head. "Although, they aren't as powerful as I am, so they might not even realize what you're doing."

With those words, she opened the door at the top of the stairs. When they turned to thank her, she was gone.

"Was she even here?" Cole asked, his eyes darting around them.

"Don't be silly," Vanna told him as she moved through the doorway. The transformation from the stark underground quarters to the upper floor was almost disorienting. One moment they were stepping off the last stair, and the next they were standing in a room that shouldn't have fit inside the dimensions of the mobile home they'd entered hours earlier.

Lin, with her elegant silver curls pinned back and her long, flowing tunic catching the soft lamplight, greeted them with a warm smile. She took them on a small tour of her home before showing them into the dining room. The dining room looked as though it had been drawn from a dream. There were vaulted wooden beams stretched impossibly high overhead, twinkling orbs of light floated above them like a starry sky. Long tables gleamed beneath candlelit sconces carved into stone walls. It felt more like an ancient lodge hidden in a forgotten mountain than a room in a trailer.

"I figured you could use a proper meal tonight," Lin said gently as she motioned for them to sit. "And we'd like to get to know you better."

They took their seats hesitantly, their senses adjusting to the surreal change in atmosphere. The scent of fresh bread, roasted vegetables and some kind of savory stew hung in the air, grounding them in the moment despite the fantastical setting.

Jerry entered not long after, rolling up the sleeves of his faded flannel shirt, and sat across from them. He gave a small nod, watching them carefully.

"Not hungry?" he asked, his gaze falling on Telara, who was listlessly pushing her food around her plate.

She gave him a weary look. "Just got a lot on my mind."

Jerry nodded slowly. "That makes sense. You've all been through more than most grown adults could handle. That kind of strain doesn't disappear with a warm meal." He leaned back in his chair, folding his arms. "But you'll need your strength, things aren't as quiet here as they once were."

Vanna looked up at him. "What do you mean?"

He exchanged a quick look with Lin, who simply began gathering empty plates and stepping into the adjacent kitchen.

"This place," Jerry began, his tone shifting slightly, "was created as a research facility for Sanctuary a very long time ago. Sanctuary built it under the guise of a retirement community so we could research not only anomalies in the crystals but as well as a way to defeat the Shadows by discovering their origin."

"Their origin?" I.Q. asked him. Jerry nodded, and I.Q. continued, "I thought they were created by the Shadow Master."

Jerry nodded. "That is what we were led to believe."

"But you don't believe that?" Tia asked while Telara listened quietly, her mind racing with this new knowledge.

"When I knew the Shadow Master," Jerry began, only to be interrupted by Telara.

"You knew the Shadow Master?" she asked, no longer sitting idly by and listening. She was now upright and tense at his words. The others were more alert as well at this news.

Jerry nodded.

"And you knew Lucius?" I.Q. asked.

Once again, Jerry nodded.

"Just how old are you?" Cole asked, and the others were so stunned by this news that they didn't think to reprimand him for his outspoken question.

Jerry laughed. "Old enough," was his response.

"So, why are you questioning whether he created the Shadows?" Telara had many questions she wanted to ask, but she felt this one was the most important.

"It wasn't a power that he ever exhibited."

I.Q. wetted his lips before he asked, "Was there anyone who exhibited that type of power?"

Jerry shook his head. "Not that we've been able to ascertain. As I said, this is a research facility created for looking into the crystals and Shadows. As a research facility, we never worried much about any military needs."

"So, what's changed?" Tia asked him.

"We've had an influx of Shadow attacks lately; unlike anything we've seen before. Coordinated. Targeted. Not random, like they used to be. That's why Sanctuary sent you here, not just for protection, but because they don't know how to stop it."

They exchanged uneasy glances.

"So, are you saying that we're here to be tested?" Cole looked at the others who were waiting for Jerry's answer.

Jerry gave a slight smile. "No one here's to poke and prod you, if that's what you're worried about. But yes, in a way, you're here to help figure this out. You'll get some training, of course." He waved a hand vaguely. "We'll make sure of that."

"When?" Telara pressed.

Jerry raised an eyebrow at her insistence. "Soon. Tomorrow, probably. Or the next day. Depends on what the days bring." His smile didn't reach his eyes.

Lin returned, brushing her hands on a towel as she stood beside Jerry. "For now, rest. There's time to worry about the rest in the morning."

He stood and motioned towards the door that Ruby had shown them to. With a flick of his wrist, the heavy door opened, revealing the stairs that led back underground to their rooms. "Lin is right, as always. Time for sleep." He gave them a long, unreadable look. "You're not just here to keep us safe. You're here to uncover what Sanctuary can't. And if you're going to survive it, you'll need more than just training. You'll need rest and nourishment, don't skip breakfast, you'll need it."

Telara looked down the stairs then back to Jerry to say something, but he was no longer there, neither was Lin. The table was cleared and the lights dimmed. They stared at one another for a few more brief moments, before they disappeared down the stairs. The door whispered shut behind them, though no one was there to close it.

Telara lay awake, staring up at the ceiling of her borrowed room, her mind far too wired for sleep. The day had been long, strange, and full of questions she still didn't have answers to. Jerry's revelation of knowing both Zane and Lucius, came to mind about questions with no answers. Not that she was truly sure she wanted that answer, they had decided that they were just going to accept their fate, and give up on trying to save themselves.

And Jerry had to open another can of worms.

She hit her pillow in frustration as she turned onto her side, trying to process everything from the day. Jerry and Lyn's home, while on the outside looked like nothing more than a standard double-wide trailer, was anything but standard on the inside. They'd stepped through the lanai first, where Henry, the gator, greeted them.

Then after the scuffle downstairs between Gary and Dee, they were escorted upstairs by Ruby. Such an interesting old lady, they knew there had to be more about her but when they questioned Lin as she showed them more of her home, she was vague in her answers.

Inside, the space stretched far beyond what the exterior

should've allowed. The living room was cavernous, with a stone fireplace dominating one wall. Flames danced and crackled in the hearth, but the room remained cool. A scattering of oversized couches and armchairs were arranged with casual precision, creating a space that felt both cozy and vast.

One large, lounge-style chair stood out. Its seat, back, and footrest were padded with thick, earthy-toned cushions. Strange metal trays flanked both sides, glistening in the firelight. Next to it sat a smaller rocking chair, its seat padded with crocheted cushions. Curled up on it was a round, fuzzy creature that looked like a pillow, until it yawned to reveal a mouth full of tiny sharp teeth.

Lin had simply cooed, "That's my sweet baby," as if that explained everything.

A narrow hallway led to a study that Lin told them was off-limits, unless invited. Then they were seated at the table in the dining hall for dinner, where Jerry joined them. They hadn't even reached the kitchen, it was set on another level entirely, Lin claimed there wasn't anything special for them to see there.

Now, staring at the painfully average white ceiling of her room, Telara felt the emptiness settle heavier in her chest. There were no little friends playing around on the ceiling, no circles, squiggles, nor any triangles. Just a plain ceiling in a plain room, with a bed, desk, two stands, and a dresser.

It was plain boring.

With another frustrated sigh, she pulled the blanket tight around her shoulders and closed her eyes. Her body felt numb, and her mind too exhausted to sort through the swirls of emotion. All she wanted was sleep.

The clinking of glass dragged her from unconsciousness.

She groaned, tugging at her blanket, only to find it gone. She opened her eyes to see her room was also gone, and looked around to see marble all around her. She felt a smooth, cool bench beneath her and tall arched ceilings loomed overhead that glimmered faintly with light that didn't come from any visible source.

Kyler stood a few feet away, hunched over a crystal bowl. Vials of colored dust and shimmering liquids were arranged before her. She poured one, then another with silver fluid into the bowl. It hissed and sparked, a soft plume of iridescent steam curling into the air as she stirred the mixture with a glass spoon.

Kyler didn't look up as she spoke. "About time you showed up, I thought you were avoiding me."

"I am," Telara muttered. She didn't sit up, just turned her face to the side and sighed. "Why don't you just leave me alone."

Kyler finally looked at her, eyebrow raised. "Leave you alone? I thought you were trying to stop the one behind the shadows."

Telara gave a tired shrug. "What does it matter? We're all going to die anyway. Maybe that's what we were meant for."

That got Kyler's attention. She crossed the distance quickly, her expression unreadable. "Where is this coming from?"

Telara gave another shrug but stayed quiet.

"If you don't learn from the past," Kyler said, voice soft but stern, "you're doomed to repeat it. Everything you've been through, everything you've learned, will mean nothing."

Telara gave a dry, humorless laugh. "Good luck with the next set of Guardians then."

"You're not even going to try?" Kyler asked.

"Nope."

"You'd rather lie there and give up?"

Telara didn't open her eyes. "Pretty much. I'm tired of people hijacking my dreams, yanking me around like a puppet, and expecting me to jump when they say jump. I'm not your pawn. Go find someone else."

A tense silence followed.

Then Kyler said coldly, "What if I decided to end your life? And the lives of your friends?"

Telara didn't flinch. "Not like our days aren't already numbered. You'll have to try harder than that. I don't care anymore."

Kyler stayed silent, but Telara didn't care.

The marble bench softened suddenly, warming beneath her.

Telara opened her eyes. She was back in her bed at Jerry and Lin's. She blinked at the ceiling, stunned. She hadn't expected to win. Not against Kyler. Not that easily.

"Good morning."

Lin greeted them warmly as they ascended the staircase leading to the main level. The rich scent of sizzling breakfast filled the air, wrapping around them like an embrace. I.Q.'s stomach growled audibly.

A deep chuckle came from behind them. They turned to see Jerry approaching, a mischievous twinkle in his eye. "Lin's cooking gets me every time too." He clapped a hand on I.Q.'s shoulder, firm and familiar, before stepping past them. "Come on, let's get seated. After breakfast, I'll give you the grand tour of our humble establishment."

"Tour?" Telara's voice cut through the air, edged with suspicion.

Jerry glanced down at her, then gave a nod. "Of course. If you're going to protect this place, you should know what you're protecting."

"And training?" Telara asked him. "We're still supposed to be training as well, correct? We're not just here to play tourist. You said so yourself last night, that we'll need rest and nourishment for what we will have to face," she challenged him.

Jerry didn't bristle, though his gaze lingered on her a moment longer. "And I meant every word I said last night, but I also said that you'll need more than just training. It's not enough to practice your powers in a safe space, you need to understand the world you're protecting, the threats you're up against, and the people you're fighting for. Real training means adapting to real-world conditions."

He stepped into the dining room and claimed the seat at the head of the long wooden table, waiting for them to follow. "Besides," he added, "you'll need fuel for the day."

They followed and took their seats. Lin was already setting platters on the table. Eggs, fresh fruit, toasted bread, and steaming mugs of coffee and tea. Jerry looked at her. "Thank you, Lin. Everything smells amazing."

Lin smiled back at him warmly. "Just trying to keep everyone standing."

Telara mumbled a quiet "thanks," not lifting her eyes from her plate. The others followed suit, offering more audible gratitude, but there was a strange quiet between them as they ate. To Telara, it felt almost surreal.

Jerry and Lin sat chatting like old friends discussing garden plans, not like people hosting a group of young warriors expected to train for their possible deaths. The dissonance made her stomach twist, though the food was incredible, her appetite faded quickly.

Afterward, they helped clear the dishes, putting them in a plastic bin that Lin had there for that purpose. When they offered to carry them to the kitchen, Lin told them not to worry, someone would be along to take care of that. Telara gave her a faint, almost apologetic smile.

Then Jerry clapped his hands once and gestured to the door. "Come on, time to stretch your legs. We usually take a cart, but we're all young and spry here, right?"

Cole's eyes flicked to Jerry's silver-streaked hair. "Right. But say, hypothetically, what if one of us wasn't quite spry enough to make it? Not naming names." He attempted to look innocent.

Jerry arched a brow, lips twitching.

Nice going, Cole. Chad's voice spoke in their minds. *If Telara doesn't offend them with her gloom, you'll do it with your mouth.*

Hey! Telara shot Chad a glare.

I'd rather ask now than figure it out after Grandpa keels over, Cole smirked inwardly.

Jerry chuckled, making them wonder if he could hear their internal conversation. "If one of you can't make the walk, we'll radio for the cart. No shame in it."

"Hardy har har," Cole muttered, though a few of the others cracked smiles. Even Telara's lips twitched slightly.

They followed Jerry outside into the Florida morning, the warmth already beginning to rise from the concrete paths.

"Arcadia is one of the few places the Arions can retire to once they've left active duty," Jerry explained as they walked. "We're still connected to Sanctuary, but it's optional. Many of us keep our ties... loosely." He gestured around at the peaceful homes lining the path. "This place started as a research center. Still is. We study crystal properties, track Shadow incursions, and try to get ahead of the darkness among many other things. What you're protecting isn't just people, but knowledge. Knowledge Sanctuary doesn't have."

That got a few glances from the Guardians. Even Telara's shoulders stiffened.

Jerry continued as if he hadn't noticed. "Also happens to be built around one of the largest golf courses in Florida."

"Wait, really?" I.Q. looked up, visibly impressed.

Jerry grinned. "Eighteen holes. Playing the full course can take a whole day, sometimes longer, if you're easily distracted."

"Longer than a day?" I.Q. frowned, skeptical.

Jerry shrugged. "You'll see."

Just then, Cole let out a loud yelp and jumped behind Chad. The other Guardians turned to frown at him, though Jerry turned casually to see a large gator amble out from behind a hedge, unbothered and stately.

"Hey there, Henry!" Jerry called out cheerfully. "Where've you been?"

"Does he have a frog in his mouth?" Vanna squinted, leaning in.

"Van!" Tia hissed, pulling her back by her arm. "You were going to look into that gator's mouth? Are you crazy?"

Vanna blinked. "I swear I saw a frog."

Jerry chuckled. "That's Peter. He likes to ride with Henry."

"In his mouth?" Vanna looked horrified. "Wouldn't Henry eat him?"

"They're best friends." Jerry said it like it was the most natural thing in the world.

They kept walking, though most of them gave Henry a wide berth. Vanna, on the other hand, walked right beside him like she belonged there.

"These homes you see," Jerry gestured again, "are where many of Sanctuary's retired operatives live. It's a place without snow, without Shadows, at least, we try to keep it that way. The recent Shadow attacks have put some of our residents on edge." He grimaced.

"No snow, but you get hurricanes every year," I.Q. pointed out, eyeing the palm trees as they passed.

Jerry nodded. "Pros and cons, kid. No place is perfect."

"True," Telara said softly, her voice more thoughtful than sarcastic this time.

Jerry gave her a sideways glance but said nothing. They kept walking through Arcadia, listening as Jerry described life in Arcadia for the semi-retired Arions. It sounded almost ideal, though they knew it was life that wasn't optional for them.

They had just passed a wide-open field where a few older residents were doing gentle stretches under the supervision of a cheerful woman in blue scrubs when Jerry turned sharply onto a narrower path.

"This way," he said, voice a little quieter now. "Fewer folks come out here, but I want you to see the full grounds. Can't defend what you don't understand."

The air felt heavier as they walked, the sounds of birds and rustling leaves seeming to muffle slightly. Ahead, the buildings were fewer and farther apart. One in particular stood out, an old utility building made of sun-bleached concrete, tucked behind a cluster of overgrown palmettos.

"What's that?" Chad asked, pointing to it.

Jerry slowed, his gait more cautious now. "Old research wing. Was shut down after a containment breach about a year ago."

"What kind of breach?" I.Q. asked, brows raised.

Jerry's lips pressed into a line. "Crystal instability. Something...we didn't expect." He stopped at the chain-link fence that enclosed the building. The gate was locked with a thick padlock, but that didn't stop them from seeing the black scorch marks streaked up the walls, jagged and uneven, like lightning strikes trapped in mid-explosion.

"Holy crap," Cole muttered. "Looks like someone tried to blow the place sky-high."

"Was this due to crystal essence?" I.Q. asked him. "Sanctuary had that problem before but Telara helped them out with that, with the help of her Rotary, of course."

"It wasn't an explosion," Jerry shook his head. "At least, not one we can explain. Energy surge, maybe. Some of the researchers in that wing claimed they saw things before it happened, shadows moving in the walls, reflections that didn't follow them."

Telara's skin prickled. She stepped a little closer to the fence, peering in. The windows of the building were blacked out with thick metal sheets, and something about the stillness around it felt wrong. There were no birds singing here, no insects buzzing, just silence.

"Did anyone get hurt?" Telara asked, her jaw tightening.

"Two researchers vanished. Their rooms were untouched, belongings still there. No signs of struggle, just... gone." Jerry's voice had lost its earlier warmth. "That was the last time anyone was allowed in."

"Why are we seeing this?" Telara asked, her voice low.

"Because you need to know what you're really protecting. Arcadia isn't just some sunny retirement home," Jerry said. "We've got knowledge here that the Shadow Master would destroy if he could, or twist to his purposes."

Vanna stepped forward, her gaze thoughtful. "Are you still studying the crystals that caused this?"

Jerry didn't answer right away. "We're being careful now, but the research continues, it has to."

"Sanctuary allows that?" Telara frowned at him.

"We operate outside of Sanctuary," Jerry informed her. "We don't answer to them, but we do share many of our discoveries with them."

"Claw would love to work here," Chance chuckled.

Jerry opened his mouth to say something when a low, metallic thud echoed from inside the building.

They all froze.

"Was that-?" Tia started but another thud stopped her. This thud was closer and also followed by a scraping sound, like something being dragged across concrete.

"Back," Jerry said quietly, raising a hand to hold them in place. "Stay behind me."

For a long moment, the group stood still. Then there was silence. Nothing more.

After a tense beat, Jerry turned to them. "This place has a way of reminding you that safety is temporary. Come on." He started walking briskly back toward the main path. "You've seen enough of this part."

They followed him, glancing over their shoulders as they went. All but Telara. She didn't look back, she didn't want to see what might be watching them from behind the sealed windows.

$$8$$

IT WAS midday before they arrived at Lumenhall, the main hub of Arcadia, the same place they'd first arrived when they'd crossed over. They had been walking quietly since their experience with the old research wing, a decrepit old building that was situated all on its own, away from the other buildings of Arcadia.

Along the way, they passed many mobile homes. Some pristine with wind chimes singing in the breeze and potted flowers spilling from porch rails, while others had mismatched siding or lawn ornaments that looked like they hadn't moved in years. One had a satellite dish duct-taped to a metal pole. Another had one of those tiny free library boxes on a post out front labeled "Magical Misfits and Gardening Tips." A few homes were shaped oddly. One was built in a dome, another in a stack of staggered cubes, defying all logic. But this was Arcadia, after all.

The residents had been just as memorable.

They'd met a wiry old man in bright orange suspenders who challenged Cole to a race and actually won, although it was close. Cole glared at Chad who fell to the ground laughing. "Why don't you race him?" Cole challenged but the old man had already moved on to find a new challenge. A grandmotherly woman with neon blue hair had tugged I.Q. into a chair and insisted on knitting him a scarf "for his aura." Two little girls ran up to them laughing and squealing, in their hands they each held a frog that looked as if they were painted with pink and yellow sparkles.

Those moments had helped, a little, but the heaviness hadn't gone away.

Now, they stood near a pond behind Lumenhall, its surface as smooth as glass except for the lazy swirls of koi and strange, glowing creatures that zipped through the water like living streaks of starlight. Thin, eel-like beings with translucent fins that shimmered in color when they passed through shadow.

"So," Jerry said as he stopped beside them, hands in his pockets, eyes on the pond. "What do you think of our modest home?"

"Interesting," Telara said flatly, staring into the water.

"That's one word for it," Chance muttered. He knelt by the pond, brushing a finger across its surface. Water followed the movement, swirling up in a slow spiral before breaking into delicate, weightless patterns, dancing through the air at his will.

Jerry watched the display in silence, unreadable.

Telara turned to him, her patience thinning. "Your home is nothing short of unique," she admitted, "but we were told our training was lacking and we weren't to deviate from it."

"Who told you that?" Jerry asked, still watching Chance and the dancing water.

"The Leaders," Telara told him, watching him.

He glanced up now, his brow furrowing. "They said that, exactly?"

Telara wrapped her arms around her torso. "We were told we could never go home. That our families don't even remember us. All we're here to do is train for the Magine.

That's all we have left. So, no offense, but we don't have time for nature walks or tourist stops."

"You sound like you've already given up," Jerry said, frowning.

Telara snorted. "What do we have left to fight for? We'll protect you if a Shadow attack happens but Ira said during our downtime that you'd help us in our training."

Jerry sighed deeply. "Well, we certainly wouldn't want him to look like a liar."

And with that, he shoved her straight into the pond.

The splash echoed around them. Chance yelped and fell backward with wide eyes while the others just stared. Telara emerged, sputtering and dripping, a lily pad stuck to her head. She slapped it off and glared daggers at Jerry. The colorful fish darted away from her in a panic.

"Why did you do that?" she demanded.

Jerry only raised a brow. "Why did you let me?"

Chance lifted her out of the water with a wave of his hand, the water rising beneath her and depositing her gently onto the grass. Cole and Tia quickly dried her with focused bursts of heat and air. Vanna winced at Telara's hair, which now stood in frizzy defiance of gravity. They watched her with apprehension.

Still glaring, Telara ran her fingers through her hair. "A little warning next would've been nice."

Jerry stepped closer. "You think your enemy's going to give you a warning?"

The question stung more than the water. Telara's retort faltered on her lips.

"You've been taught to fight," Jerry said, softer now. "You know your powers. You've faced Shadows and survived. But training doesn't happen in a vacuum. You need to learn how to live in the world you're trying to save. That's the difference between surviving and enduring."

"Why?" Telara asked, her voice breaking just a little. "We're just going to die anyway."

"Is that what you truly believe?" Jerry asked gently.

She didn't answer right away. "It's what we were told. Every Guardian that came before us has died. Everyone who tried to help us is either gone or have turned against us. Our lives have been rewritten and our families are now erased. This isn't hope, it's a sentence." She turned away, her wet clothes clinging to her as she marched away from them. "When you're ready to train us, let me know. I'm done with sightseeing."

The others lingered, giving Jerry uncertain, apologetic looks. Then, one by one, they followed after her. Jerry stood there a while longer, staring into the pond as the glowing creatures slipped back into their quiet dance.

If breakfast had been quiet, then dinner was a tomb.

After Jerry shoved Telara into the pond, they weren't sure if it had been a lesson or a reminder that they weren't really in control of their lives, so they walked back to Jerry and Lin's home in strained silence. Even the sounds of nature seemed hesitant, as if the world itself sensed the weight they carried on their shoulders.

Once inside, they scattered like leaves in the wind, each disappearing into their assigned rooms without a word to one another. It wasn't anger they felt, more like fatigue, confusion, bruised egos, and hearts trying to shield themselves from pain.

They didn't mention the pond, nor the glowing creatures they saw in there. Nothing said about the way Telara marched off with her hair still dripping.

It wasn't until Lin summoned them for dinner that they slowly emerged from their rooms. They moved like faded echoes of who they once were, going through the motions of sitting, eating, and chewing, but without conversation or warmth. Even Lin's food, savory roasted vegetables and thick slices of buttery cornbread, barely stirred appetites. The clink of utensils scraping across plates filled the room, louder than it had any right to be.

Jerry said nothing about the pond and neither did they, they said nothing actually. Lin watched them, with eyes that seemed to see more than she let on. She'd speak lightly about others that lived in Arcadia, telling Jerry about a request from Betty who had put in a requisition for some lab supplies that she needed for one of her projects. Jerry nodded to Lin. "I will make sure Betty gets what she needs."

Lin placed her petite hand on top of his with a smile. "I know you will, dear. I told her as much."

When dinner ended, they started to head in the direction of their rooms, before they even reached the door, Jerry spoke. "We'll talk in the morning."

His words weren't harsh, but they were definite. The group paused mid-step but didn't turn to face him. Telara gave a slow nod, then they continued through the doorway and down the stairs silently to their rooms.

They walked past the Social Room where they could hear Dee dressing down someone who dared to try to help her, they weren't sure why anyone would try to help someone who acted so shrewish. Vanna and the guys stopped to peer into the room, curious who the victim was. Telara and Tia moved down the hallway towards their rooms, Telara had been about to open the door to her room when Tia's voice floated softly to her.

"Telara..."

Telara turned to see Tia leaning against the doorframe to her room with her arms wrapped around herself, her eyes troubled. Telara leaned back against her door silently and waited for Tia to speak.

"I don't feel right about this," Tia said quietly. "Jerry and Lin have been nothing but kind to us. I don't want to be rude to them."

Telara's shoulders tensed, her voice sounded tired, but not cold. "I'm not trying to be rude, Tia. I just can't keep pretending that this is… normal. That this place is safe or that we can just be grateful tourists when we're being trained to die."

Tia looked down, breathing in deeply. "I know. I miss my mom's garden," she murmured. "The smell of jasmine in the evenings. I miss my dad's bad singing and burnt pancakes. But they don't remember me anymore. None of them do."

Telara's expression softened, guilt creeping in. "I know. I miss Ra, as twins we were never as close as other twins, but we still loved one another." She breathed in deeply. "I miss being someone who mattered to people who knew my name before all of this. But missing it doesn't bring it back."

Tia nodded. "Still… I hate how cold we've become. I don't want to be like one of the past Guardians they told us about, who have no friends except for each other."

"It does make it so that I now understand why they were that way," Telara said as she ran her fingers along her door-frame. "If they had known they weren't expected to live past that battle, why would they want to have friends."

Behind them, quiet footsteps echoed in the hallway as the others joined them.

"I still want to feel," Tia said with a sad smile.

"I think we're all feeling that," Vanna said gently, leaning against the wall. "I laughed today when those kids showed us their frogs with such excitement. I forgot, for like five seconds, that we're supposed to be weapons."

"We're not weapons," Chad muttered, leaning his chin on Vanna's shoulder. "We're just kids who didn't get a choice."

"I don't want to hurt anyone," Telara whispered. "Not Jerry, not Lin, not the people here or back in Sanctuary. I'm too scared to get close to anyone. What happens when we go to fight the Magine and don't make it back? Do they get added to the list of people who mourn us, then forget us until the next set of Guardians come along?" Her lips pulled into a wry smile that showed no humor.

There was silence, broken only by the sound of Cole clearing his throat and rubbing the back of his neck awkwardly. "We're all on edge. Telara, you're not wrong for being angry." He looked over at Tia who watched him with a curious expression. "And you're not wrong, Tia, for wanting to be friendly. I guess... I just wish there was someone who could tell us how to be both."

Telara stared at Cole, momentarily at a loss for words. He was usually the flirt, the class clown. Quick with a smirk or sarcastic jab, not thoughtful insight. But the calm weight behind his words carried a surprising depth, a wisdom that didn't match his usual carefree persona. It was a stark reminder of how serious things had become, enough to pull something real from even Cole. The others seemed just as caught off guard, their stunned expressions mirroring her own. The unexpected shift helped to ease some of her frustration, grounding her more than she'd expected.

She sighed, turned and opened her door to her room, and stepped inside. "Good night," she told them softly. Her heart felt heavy, they'd been through so much together, and it wasn't over. They were her friends and they were her family, at least they'd never lose one another, at least until the very end.

One by one, the others slipped into their rooms as well. Doors clicked softly shut. Outside, the moon hung over Arcadia like a pale eye watching a chessboard. Still and silent, waiting for the next move.

9

Telara's hands trembled as she pulled back the covers. Keeping her emotions in check around others had her feeling the strain when she finally could be by herself. She could feel the others' concerns through their link; she attempted to send reassurances to them but they felt flat to even her. After graduation they'd all agreed, no emotions for anyone to see. Keep it locked down and stay focused, even numb. That was beginning to tax them all.

How do you stay calm when all you want to do is scream, cry, laugh, or just even disappear?

She slid under the covers and let her eyes fall shut, whispering a desperate prayer to anyone that would listen, that her sleep would be uninterrupted tonight.

A prayer that was ignored.

"About time." Kyler's voice sliced through the quiet like broken glass. When Telara stayed where she was, not moving or speaking, Kyler's voice showed aggravation. "Are you going to lay there like a sulking child or speak to me?"

Telara kept her eyes closed and her voice showed none of the churning emotions that she held within, or at least she liked to think it didn't. "If I'm such a bother, send me back to my room and let me enjoy the silence."

"I'm willing to overlook your earlier tantrum," Kyler told her coolly, "but don't test me, Guardian. Patience isn't a luxury I often extend."

That did it. Telara sat up and glared at her. "Or what? What else can you take from me that hasn't already been stripped away?" Her voice cracked with the raw edge of grief. "My family's gone. My future? Already promised to a battlefield. So go ahead. Threaten me. Kill me. Just stop pretending like this is some kind of favor."

Kyler didn't flinch. Her haughty gaze remained steady, arms crossed in that infuriating, smug calm. "And yet you still care. You're here, yelling at me, asking questions. You haven't given up."

"Maybe not completely," Telara admitted bitterly. "But I'm done being used. Everyone wants something from us. Even you."

"Is it so wrong to want something in return?" Kyler stepped forward, her expression genuinely curious. "I help you discover who you truly are, you become who you were always meant to be. You can learn how to stop the traitor, that will help you, will help your friends and this place you call home. You could be the one who ends this all, be the hero."

"You only care because it helps you get what you want," Telara said flatly. "Even if you won't admit what it is that you're looking for. You don't care about us. If you did, you'd have helped the others before us."

Kyler's lips curled in a half-smile. "They were weak. Their bloodlines diluted. Nothing but cannon fodder."

With a wave of her hand, she summoned a garden just beyond the earthen doorway. Telara followed, more out of habit than interest, until she saw it. A crystalline oasis shimmered in the night. Towering crystal flowers pulsed with inner light. At the garden's center stood a massive crystal, larger even than the Parent Crystals in Sanctuary. Light shimmered through its core, while a strange darkness clung to the base like a parasite.

For a moment, Telara forgot her anger.

A sharp shriek broke the stillness. She turned just in time to see Kyler casually spraying a tiny winged creature. A crystal-winged pixie. It writhed and fell, gasping.

"Stop!" Telara rushed forward.

Kyler sprayed another. "They steal my crystals," she said without emotion. "They're pests."

Telara caught the second one with her power, but it was too late. She cradled the tiny creature as it died in her hand, tears rising to her eyes.

"It wasn't a pest. It was alive. It mattered."

Kyler rolled her eyes and swatted the first dead pixie off one of her crystal flowers. "You're too sentimental. That'll get you killed."

"No, you have no empathy," Telara snapped, her voice shaking. "You talk about the truth, but you're no better than the monsters we're fighting. You only value life when it serves you."

"Power is what matters," Kyler replied coldly. "Without it, you're just dust waiting to scatter. Like those pixies. Like the Guardians who came before you."

Telara's jaw clenched. "Why me, then? Why help me if you didn't care before?"

"Because you can fix what's been broken," Kyler said, her voice threading with urgency now. "You can mend the realms, restore what was lost. The Paladins- "

"What do you know about the Paladins?" Telara interrupted sharply.

Kyler waved her off. "What I know isn't important. What you need to know is buried in your past. You need to go back again. That's where the answers lie."

"And what good are answers if we can't survive the Shadows long enough to use them?"

Kyler sighed with frustration. "The Shadows are a distraction. They aren't your true enemy."

"They're trying to kill us." Telara's voice dropped to a whisper. "I'm not asking for you to hold our hands, all I'm asking is for honesty."

"Then here it is," Kyler said, voice sharp again. "You'll only win if you learn to control them. Make them bend to your will. Show them your true power."

"I've already mastered my powers," Telara argued. "And none of them control shadows."

Kyler's tone turned mocking. "Then maybe you're not as powerful as you think."

Telara's fists clenched. "You drag me here, dangle cryptic promises, and expect obedience? If you truly believe in your cause, tell me the whole truth. What're you hiding?"

Kyler hesitated, just a flicker, but Telara saw it. It was small and Kyler recovered quickly, but it was there. "Do you want to save your friends or not?" Kyler hit back.

Telara didn't blink. "I want to stop being your pawn."

Darkness engulfed her. When she opened her eyes, she was back in her room. "For someone so powerful," she muttered into the silence, "you sure do crumble fast when the truth hits back." She turned her back on the world, and for once, didn't beg for a dreamless sleep. She was too tired to hope for peace anymore.

"True powers?" I.Q. echoed, frowning thoughtfully as they made their way up the stairs to breakfast.

Telara nodded, her voice weary. "That's what she said. Like the powers we know and use aren't enough."

"That doesn't even make sense," Tia said, brushing a hand

through her hair. "Is she saying your telekinesis isn't your real power?"

Telara shrugged. "Your guess is as good as mine."

"So… we all have hidden powers just waiting to pop out?" Chad's eyes lit up, the idea clearly appealing.

"Don't start planning your superhero name just yet," Telara muttered. "Consider the source. Kyler's great at riddles and not much else."

"She's useless," Chance said flatly.

"She's worse than useless," Telara corrected, voice tightening. "She's deliberately cryptic. Tells you just enough to keep you dangling, and not one word more."

"Why does she only come to you?" Cole asked. "Why not visit the rest of us in our dreams?"

Telara gave him a long, exasperated look. "Because I clearly pissed off the universe somewhere along the way."

"She keeps bringing up crystals," I.Q. said, clearly trying to steer things back on track. "And the realms. She talks like everything's about the crystals, as if they belong to her."

"They probably do," Telara muttered, rubbing at her temples.

"Think the crystals are the key to healing the realms?" I.Q. asked. "Could they really be tied to all of this?"

Telara raised a hand and patted I.Q. on his shoulder. "Tell you what. Next dream is all yours. You can ask her yourself."

"I don't think that's how it works," I.Q. said dryly.

"A girl can dream, can't she?" Telara muttered.

"You sure can." Cole told her. "Just not without someone irritating you in that dream."

Telara grimaced.

"Have you tried asking her more direct questions?" Cole offered.

Telara turned a sharp look on him. "Yes. Have you ever tried talking to a being who thinks riddles are a valid form of communication?"

"She doesn't sound very customer-service friendly," Chance remarked.

"That's one way to put it," Telara snorted.

Vanna, quieter than usual, spoke up. "But what if the crystals are a way to end this war, with us surviving?"

Telara's expression softened, but her voice was grim. "Haven't we already given up on that?"

"Why should we?" Vanna asked, surprising them all with her quiet insistence. "Why give up now?"

"Because it hurts too much to keep hoping," Telara replied after a long breath. "Every time we think we've found something, a new spell, a lead, a possible win, it just... breaks apart. I'm tired of getting my hopes up."

The group went quiet, Vanna nodded slowly as the air turned heavy with shared weight.

"Well, Kyler's definitely obsessed with crystals," Chance offered into the silence.

"She's got a whole garden of them," Chad added.

Telara grimaced. "I know."

"Hmmmm," I.Q. murmured, his fingers absently tapping the worn spine of the book in his hand.

"What's up, I.Q.?" Tia asked.

He looked at Telara, thoughtful. "Back in Haven, the book mentioned Crystal Lords, Crystal Keepers, and Crystal Seers. Remember?"

They all nodded.

"Kyler called herself a Crystal Keeper."

"She did," Telara confirmed with a nod, then grimaced. "A Crystal Keeper who kills pixie-like creatures who dare to enter her garden."

"Charming," Cole muttered.

"I think we need to learn more about what those titles actually mean," I.Q. said. "There has to be a reason that she wants Telara focused on the crystals."

"Hopefully you can get better answers than me," Telara

said bitterly. "Kyler only tells me what she wants me to know, and sometimes I feel as if that isn't very much."

"Well, maybe the answers are in here," I.Q. held up the book. "Maybe the truth, or at least part of it, is buried in this old text."

"Or maybe it's another rabbit hole that leads nowhere," Telara muttered.

"Maybe," I.Q. admitted. "But I'd rather chase a maybe than sit around doing nothing."

"At least when we were trying, we weren't all so..." Tia hesitated, then continued softly, "...so broken."

Telara didn't respond, but she didn't pull away from the hand Tia placed gently on her shoulder.

The group moved up the last few steps into the warm, welcoming main room. The smell of breakfast greeted them, and Lin stood waiting near the table, a kind smile on her face. They looked around but they didn't see Jerry, it was just them and Lin there.

"Jer's tied up in meetings this morning," Lin told them, gesturing for them to sit. "Our granddaughter and her friends will be arriving shortly to escort you to Lumenhall. That's where you'll find Arcadia's training rooms, there's also Hallowmere Door. That's where many here like to eat, drink, and trade stories. You'll find some interesting characters there." She gave them an encouraging smile.

They murmured their thanks as they sat down to eat. Telara moved slowly to her seat, her eyes darting to the book that I.Q. held. She wondered if maybe that book would give them the answers that Kyler wouldn't.

10

"Gramps said to make sure you guys take a break," Lillie announced with that impish smile of hers.

The Guardians stood panting in one of the vast training chambers deep beneath Lumenhall. The room, like many others in this underground world, was carved from ancient stone and pulsing gently with arcane light. After breakfast with Lin, the Vanguards had brought them below the clubhouse of Arcadia, into the hidden heart of Lumenhall, a sprawling, enchanted underworld that felt more like a forgotten kingdom than a base.

What lay beneath was astounding, a network of interwoven halls and vaults, each shimmering with its own strange energy. Training arenas ranged from illusion-warped battlefields to elemental gauntlets where fire rained sideways and gravity bent at will. Towering vaults held ancient weaponry and enchanted armories, while lower levels pulsed with energy from hidden ley lines. They had followed the Vanguards, listening to them as they gestured around them and explained all they saw.

But it wasn't just combat facilities they saw, they also passed crystalline observatories where researchers studied the crystals used by Sanctuary and others. They said they were even charting how the crystals resonated with the Guardians' abilities, something that was new to them. Why would they be charting that? What did it even matter when they wouldn't be around for long? They had looked at each other but pursed their lips together, their unspoken questions kept at bay.

They walked past other laboratories where they saw containment chambers warded with old magic where captured Shadow creatures writhed in stasis, studied under harsh blue light. They also saw a dozen circular chambers, like petals on a flower, that served as laboratories and theoretical halls. Some focused on energy alchemy, others on deciphering ancient prophecies tied to the crystals and a darkness that could only be the rise of the Shadows and their master.

Every home nestled in the lower realm of Lumenhall connected to these corridors as well as those above. The corridors of Lumenhall showed a labyrinth of magic and purpose. They were in a place of living knowledge, evolving magic, and mystery.

They hadn't yet seen Hallowmere Door, the legendary meeting hall where all paths were said to converge, but the Vanguards had pointed down a corridor that pulsed with warm light and laughter drifting from beyond a carved silverwood arch.

Instead, they had been shown to a training chamber the size of a cathedral, where they could program and shape the environment to their needs. They'd spent the last five hours dodging phantom arrows, sprinting over illusionary collapsing bridges, and fighting off golems forged from enchanted stone and spirit flame. The dummies they battled came alive with snarling enchantments and cunning mimicry. The room adapted to their abilities, testing them, provoking them.

Now they stood, sweating and aching, glancing at their watches with groans.

"We're the Guardians. We don't need no stinking break," Cole gasped, trying to deepen his voice, but his exhaustion made the impression fall flat.

"Well, my gramps runs Arcadia," Lillie said, arms crossed, her smirk fierce and adorable, "and he said you need to take a break."

Kasey, Jacob, Allison, and Carter stood behind her, clearly amused. "And we're here to make sure you do," Kasey added.

"If Jerry wants a break, he can take a break," Tia muttered as she vaulted over a stone golem in mid-charge. She spun, using its own momentum to hurl it into a wall with a loud crack. As it staggered back to its feet, a creeping sheen of frost formed around its legs. In seconds, it was encased in ice.

"I had it, you know," she said, throwing Chad a dark look.

Chad grinned, ignoring the dark look. "I just wanted to join the fun."

The golem burst free with a roar, shards of ice scattering. Tia raised a brow towards Chad, who just shrugged his shoulders.

"Let a pro handle this," Cole shouted, flames igniting across his body. He launched himself at the golem, gripping its stone neck. Fire engulfed them both until the creature collapsed into a pool of steaming goo at Cole's feet. He turned with a grin. "See?"

"Ummm… Cole?" Vanna pointed. "Your feet."

He looked at his feet, his eyes widening. The molten golem goo was creeping up his legs like living tar. "Hey! Hey!" he yelled, trying to reignite his fire, but the slime was siphoning his energy. His flames dimmed. "Get this thing off me!" He started hitting the goo with his nun chucks, they still carried their flames but did nothing against the goo.

Chance shot a jet of water at him, but the heat from Cole's

body and nun chucks turned it to steam. I.Q. followed with arcs of electricity, but they fizzled out on contact.

The goo reached Cole's neck. Panic flashed in his eyes.

"Enough!" Vanna dropped to her knees and pressed her palms to the floor. The earth trembled, then rose into the form of a giant bear covered in moss and glowing runes. It lumbered forward and absorbed the golem into itself, dissolving the goo and freeing Cole.

"I'd say Jerry was right," Kasey observed dryly, looking over at Jacob who nodded in agreement, his lips quirking up in a grin.

"Grandpa knows best," Lillie chimed, drawing laughter from Allison and Carter.

"Yeah, well, he's not a Guardian," Telara muttered. With a flick of her hand, she stopped a volley of conjured projectiles mid-air, letting them fall harmlessly to the ground. She looked over at the Vanguards. "When you're a Guardian, it's different."

"Hmph." Kasey pushed off the wall and walked forward. "Pam said you were different from the past Guardians. Guess she was wrong."

"Listen, kid…" Telara began, her voice low. She stepped forward, ignoring the tense glances from Vanna and Tia. "We're the ones walking into our own funeral. Let us do it in peace."

Kasey's eyes narrowed. Behind her, the other Vanguards shifted uncomfortably. "I thought Pam was working on a way to prevent that," Kasey said.

Telara paused. It seemed not everyone had been told about Pam's defection. Sanctuary still clung to its secrets, even from its own. But it wasn't their place to explain or defend. "She's gone," Telara finally said. "And we lost our families. Now all we've got is training… and a short lifespan."

"You lost your families?" Allison whispered, her eyes wide.

"Yeah," Vanna said softly with a small nod.

"The leaders took them from us," Cole added. The sorrow in his voice lingered like smoke.

"Aren't you the Guardians?" Allison asked them.

"Yeah," I.Q. answered, folding his arms. Tia and Telara looked at each other but said nothing, waiting to see where this conversation was going.

"Don't you have powers that others don't?" Carter asked them.

"Yeah," Chance answered slowly, his brows furrowed.

"So… how can they tell you what to do?" Lillie asked, her hands linked in front of her, looking like a smaller version of Jerry.

Tia glanced at Telara, who remained silent. So, Tia spoke up instead. "Because there's so much that we still don't know."

"Then learn it," Kasey said plainly. "Then you can get your families back."

"Not that easy, kiddos," Chad replied, his voice low.

"Why?" Kasey asked.

"The Shadow Master is coming," I.Q. said. "And we're the only ones who can stop him."

"Then learn what you don't know," Allison told them.

"Learn your powers," Carter added.

"Defeat the Shadow Master and stay alive," Lillie spoke up.

"Then you get your families back," Kasey finished, stepping closer.

"Sounds so easy," Telara scoffed.

"It can be," Allison said gently. "You're the ones holding yourselves back."

"Without Pam, we don't know where to go," Telara admitted, her voice cracking. "She was the one who began our journey to save our lives."

"So… Pam's the only one who knows anything?" Kasey asked. When the Guardians nodded, except I.Q. who looked thoughtful, her frown deepened. "Then why didn't she tell you?"

They exchanged uneasy glances, searching for answers they didn't have.

"Maybe she's not the only one," Kasey suggested.

"Why wouldn't anyone else say anything?" Vanna asked.

"Did you ask?" Lillie tilted her head, her sharp gaze too much like Jerry's for comfort.

Telara had reached her limit. She was tired. She was tired of fighting, of losing, of the endless maze of half-truths and dead ends. "They should've come to us if they knew anything, they're supposed to be our friends," she blurted out.

Kasey snorted. "Yeah. Because you've been so approachable."

The Guardians looked at each other, then at Telara, who finally sighed and gave a small nod. "Point taken."

"Then be the Guardians Pam told us about," Kasey said. With that said, she and the others turned and left the room.

THE SOUND OF AN IRON DOOR GROANING OPEN FILLED THE STONE caverns where Hades kept Lucius prisoner. The sound sliced through the stale silence like a blade.

Lucius didn't lift his head. "What is it this time?" he muttered from his position on the cold floor. "Come to lecture me on the futility of resistance, or just another ego boost?"

Hades stepped inside the threshold, but no further. He carried no food, no threats, only a flickering orb of smoke in his hand.

"I noticed that you haven't been watching the vision portal," Hades told him as the orb started to grow.

Lucius kept his head lowered, his wrists resting on his knees while his hands rested loosely there. "The Guardians are with Jerry; he'll take care of them. I'm not in the mood to entertain you any longer, *grandpa*." He sneered out that last word.

"Don't call me that!" The god growled.

"Why not?" Lucius countered. "It's the truth, whether either of us like it or not. It's the reason you're protecting a murderer."

"If she killed anyone, she was provoked!" Hades practically yelled.

Lucius sighed. "What are you even doing here?"

"Thought you might want an update on your precious Guardians," Hades told him.

Lucius placed his hands on the ground next to him and pushed up so that he stood to face the god. "What do you mean?"

The orb twisted in Hades' hand, rising up until it fused with the empty vision portal, hazy at first, then sharpened into a familiar training room. He had been there before, he helped Jerry create Lumenhall, after all. His gaze locked on the inhabitants of the room, he watched Telara throwing herself into drills again and again, her face fierce and movements mechanical. The other Guardians twisted and evaded obstacles as they fought alongside her. The room lit up with their powers but it was the look on their faces that had his attention. So lost and forlorn, it had his throat tightening.

"They're falling apart," Lucius whispered.

Hades stayed silent, watching him.

"They've closed themselves off," Lucius said, more to himself than to his jailer. "They think they can fix it all by training harder. By pretending they don't care."

"You taught them that," Hades replied. "Control. Distance. Sacrifice."

"I taught them how to protect each other." Lucius's voice cracked as he turned away from the portal. "Not how to become hollow."

Hades crossed his arms. "Then maybe you should've prepared them for loss."

"They haven't lost me yet." Lucius's eyes burned with quiet fury. "I'm still here. Still alive."

"And yet they grieve you."

Lucius looked back at the portal. Vanna knelt on the ground, her eyes looking right at him, so full of wanting she knew she shouldn't have. A wanting to live, laugh and even love. He remembered the past Guardians, growing up in Sanctuary, all they knew was the battle. They didn't even seem real to him, they weren't the true reincarnations, so he had them trained and sent them to their deaths. Was this his penance for those deaths? Deaths he had orchestrated so that the way for the true reincarnations would be open. At the command of the god who watched him closely.

"You did this," Lucius said, voice low.

"They're still breathing," Hades said. "For now."

"They're breaking," Lucius growled. "And all I can do is watch from behind this wall while you justify it."

"Would you rather they crumble with you?" Hades stepped closer to the vision portal, eyes narrowed. "If I let you out, what happens? You reunite? You actually think you can save them?"

"I can give them a fighting chance," Lucius snapped. "Let them know that it isn't hopeless. I can tell them the truth, finally."

"And that's why you'll never leave here." Hades glowered at him.

"This is all your fault, you're the reason my family is being torn apart." Lucius glared at him.

Hades's jaw tightened. "You think I don't understand what it's like to watch your family unravel?"

"Larsa? My mother?" Lucius gave a shake of his head and sighed. "If you really love her, if you believe she can be saved, do something. Stop hiding behind cages, riddles, and excuses. She needs to atone for her crimes, what you're doing, isn't doing her any favors."

Hades looked at him, and for a moment, just a flicker, he seemed tired.

"They need me," Lucius whispered, almost pleading. "Not as a warrior. As their anchor."

Hades stood there, saying nothing for a few moments. Then, with a wave of his hand, the portal vanished. "Since you don't want to entertain me, you won't need that no more." He moved towards the prison door.

"Hades!" Lucius shouted.

"They need to stand on their own," Hades told him coldly, without turning around.

Lucius looked over at the empty wall where the images once played. "They were never meant to stand alone."

Hades started moving forward again. "Then I hope they remember how to fall." As Hades moved through the doorway, he faded from sight.

Lucius was left in the cell with no portal to watch, just the silence.

11

THAT NIGHT they were more subdued when they entered Jerry and Lin's home, the kids had given them much to think about. They just weren't sure what to do with it, not right now. Jerry was sitting in his armchair when they entered. His elbows rested on the arms while his fingers pressed together at the tips, held against his chin. They paused and looked at each other, not sure if they should say or do anything. He motioned towards the chairs and sofa. "Please take a seat." They paused briefly before they moved to sit down. "How did your training session go today?" He asked them.

They looked at each other, a few biting their lips while the others just shrugged. It was I.Q. who answered, "It felt like most training we've done at Sanctuary… except your training rooms feel supercharged. I always thought Sanctuary had the best."

I don't know. Cole spoke mentally. *I think the Prime Rooms back in Haven, leaves all branches of Sanctuary in the dust.* Telara winced at those words, they hadn't said anything about those rooms since Zane's betrayal. *I'm sorry.* Cole said but she just shook her head.

Jerry nodded at I.Q., although his eyes were watching

Cole and Telara as if he could hear their conversation. "They do have the best," he said, "but I'm guessing you haven't seen everything that Sanctuary has to offer." The Guardians sat straighter at those words. "Lumenhall was created by both myself and Lucius."

That caught their attention.

"Lucius helped create Lumenhall?" Telara asked.

Jerry nodded to her. "He did, and we opened it for all of Arcadia. But we're still an extension of Sanctuary."

"Sanctuary retirement home," Telara said.

"Yes," Jerry nodded. "But yet, so much more."

"What do you mean?" Vanna pulled her legs up to her chest where she wrapped her arms around them.

"The ones who live here are retired from Sanctuary; you've met some of them." They nodded at his words. "The children and grandchildren visit with us while we're here, they keep us informed about what's going on outside of Arcadia."

"Not everything," Cole told him.

Jerry tilted his head. "What do you mean?"

"Your granddaughter and her friends knew nothing about Pam defecting to team Shadow," Telara said. Her tone lacked its usual fire, more tired than angry.

Jerry nodded while he breathed in, "we chose to keep that quiet." He admitted.

"More secrets, just like Sanctuary," Telara's voice sounded resigned.

"Sometimes secrets are necessary," Jerry said gently, eyes steady on her. "Can you honestly tell me you've never held something back from your teammates?"

Telara dropped her gaze, saying nothing.

Jerry nodded. "I don't like secrets and I don't like lies. Secrets are sometimes necessary but I'll never lie to you. You give me your best and I'll return the favor. This isn't a game, this is reality. If you're not able to keep up, you'll get trampled."

The room went quiet. The weight of his words settled in thick around them, listening to Jerry reminded them of their time with Zane. Something that had them all feeling on edge, they thought they had a friend in him, and he ended up being the big baddie. Telara turned her gaze from looking at Vanna who still hugged her knees over to Jerry, who was watching her. They'd all been trying to keep their emotions buried, play it cool, play it numb, but Telara couldn't hold it in anymore.

"You know, you sound a lot like Zane," she confronted Jerry, her hands on her hips and her face hard. The others turned their amazed expressions to her, they hadn't expected this. "He wanted honesty from us and promised the same in return, only to betray us."

Jerry nodded. "I've been informed," he told them.

"You've been informed?" Telara asked him, her face contorted with her pain. "That doesn't mean you can understand what we've been through. That doesn't mean you know what we're going through."

"I don't," Jerry said evenly. "I won't pretend to understand the pain you've been through. I've read what happened at Haven, but I can't claim to feel it." His voice softened, but didn't lose its weight. "I'm not a therapist. I don't have the tools to heal that kind of pain. But I won't lie to you—and I won't let you lie to me, either."

When Telara snorted, he looked right at her. "You have my word."

"We don't know you well enough to know if your word means anything." Telara countered while the others pressed their lips together but said nothing.

"Well, then let me tell you about me," Jerry told them and waited to see if anyone spoke up. When no one did, he continued, "I used to be the Alpha faction leader at Sanctuary. That's where I met my Lin."

"Was she part of Sanctuary? Another faction leader?" Chance asked.

Jerry chuckled, "actually, she's a faerie princess. I met her during one of the Alpha's missions. She gave up her throne to be with me."

"Love at first sight?" Vanna asked with a dreamy expression.

Jerry laughed. "Not quite. She shrank me to the size of an ant the first time we met."

"You deserved it!" Lin's voice rang out from the other room.

Jerry's grin widened, "I might have been a little cocky."

"A little?" Lin's indignant question could be heard loud and clear.

Jerry nodded, his grin still visible. "Okay, a lot. But eventually she came to realize how lucky she was to have me." He gave a hearty laugh at the sound of Lin clearing her throat very loudly, still outside of the room. "Fine, fine, I'm the lucky one."

"Much better."

Jerry winked at his wife, then turned back to look at them. "After Lin and I got married, I handed the lead of the Alpha Faction over to my second. I worked in Citadel for many years, and we started our family. They grew up in Citadel and some have moved to other branches while we have some that have nothing to do with Sanctuary or any of its subsidies of sorts."

"When did you and Lucius create Arcadia?" I.Q. asked him.

"When I decided to retire from Citadel, but wasn't quite ready to completely retire." Jerry smiled at them. "We purchased this land and created Arcadia. We couldn't recreate the magical shield that protected Sanctuary from the outside world, but we could make Arcadia resemble a retirement community. There's a magical shield around Arcadia that keeps outsiders away, and of course there's Lumenhall."

"How many branches are there of Sanctuary?" I.Q. asked as he leaned forward on his knees.

"Exactly? I'm not sure anyone knows the exact number." Jerry gave a nonchalant lift of his shoulder. "Sanctuary has been here since the time of the ancient gods, many families have come and gone during that time. You've been introduced to the ones that you've needed to be exposed to."

"Even Haven?" Telara asked him, frowning.

Jerry nodded. "Even Haven. The highs and lows, they both shape you. You've had more lows than most, but there have been highs. Don't forget them. Without the good, the bad overwhelms you. As Guardians, you face more than most. That can define you, or destroy you. The choice is yours."

He leaned back. "I'll help you however I can—but not if you lie to me. Be honest, or I'm useless to you."

"Oh Jer, don't be so serious," Lyn walked in with a tiny dog in her arms. The dog was dark grey and silver colored; its dark eyes stared at them from Lin's arms. "They know what they're up against, I'm sure."

Jerry stood up and kissed his wife on her cheek, "yes, dear." He smiled lovingly down at her. The Guardians shifted in their seats feeling as if they were interlopers but went still when Jerry turned his sharp gaze upon them. "Don't forget my words, I'm not one to repeat myself." He still had the same genial smile on his face but his words were spoken with purpose. They nodded.

Lin smiled at Jerry petting her grey and silver dog. "Lucy is expecting you to call her, it seems the Hunters are in need of your counsel." She patted Jerry's hand when he opened his mouth, possibly to protest, but they'd never know as Lin continued. "You go talk to our girl, let them go get ready for dinner. I might even make a peanut butter pie for dessert."

"You know the words to my heart," He grinned and kissed her once more before turning to them. "I'll see you at dinner."

They nodded their heads in unison but didn't move until he disappeared from the room. Lin smiled, "go get ready for dinner while Bear helps me get the things on the table." She kissed the head of the dog in her arms.

"The dog is going to help you get the food on the table?" Cole stared at the dog with uncertainty.

Lin laughed, "no worries, there won't be any dog hair, I promise."

12

TELARA OPENED her eyes to the ceiling of Kyler's house. After several days of dreamless sleep, she had hoped Kyler had finally taken the hint and left her alone. She sighed in exasperation. She wasn't in the mood to deal with cryptic riddles and twisted dream logic tonight. If Kyler wasn't going to give them answers, she might as well let them die and be done with it.

"Where are we?"

Telara sat upright at Cole's voice and blinked. The others were here too, every Guardian sat up from pristine white benches arranged in a ring within Kyler's oddly sterile chamber. The earthen room off to the back still held the familiar wooden table covered in glinting crystals and vials of potions. Dream or not, it was unnerving to see her friends here now. At least Kyler hadn't dumped them all into the weird bedroom where Telara first arrived. That would've been harder to explain.

"Telara?" Tia's voice broke the quiet.

Telara glanced at the other's confused faces and gave a dry shrug. "Welcome to Kyler's house of horrors."

"Horrors?"

Kyler stood framed in the archway that led to the shimmering crystal garden. Her pale porcelain skin glowed with a faint lavender hue under the garden light. Her long, deep violet hair moved unnaturally, swaying like it had a mind of its own. She regarded them with those piercing, shard-like purple eyes.

"Wow!" Chad breathed out. "You weren't kidding about how purple she is."

His brother elbowed him hard.

"Ow!" Chad frowned at his brother. "What?"

"Between you and Cole, I'm surprised that we haven't been vaporized yet," Tia muttered.

"Hey!" Cole protested. "I didn't say anything this time."

"This time," Tia shot back. Cole made a face at her but she just ignored him.

"Must we endure this endless chatter?" Kyler asked in her dismissive manner. "If you guys want to learn the truth of the past then we need to move and move swiftly."

"You're going to help us survive?" I.Q. asked, curiosity layered under suspicion.

"That is your choice, only learning about the past will help you in the future." Kyler told him without even addressing him, she was good at talking to you without actually talking to you. Something that aggravated Telara to no end. "So, let's begin."

"Wait!" Telara held up her hand.

Kyler sighed and turned to look at Telara, "yes? What is it now?" The others looked at Telara with wide eyes.

"Why did you bring all of us here this time?" Telara asked her.

"Didn't you want all your friends here with you?" Kyler asked her back.

"Well, yeah," Telara started out slowly. "But I wanted that before and you didn't bring them then. So, why now?" Telara hooked her thumbs in her pockets.

"Hey T," Chance jumped up and held out his hands. "Don't question it too hard, or she might kick us out."

Kyler ignored him. "You weren't being cooperative. This is an adjustment." Her words were clipped and precise. "A test to see if you will be."

Telara shrugged her shoulders when they looked at her with matching quizzical expressions. "Now you know why I'd wake up agitated. Good luck getting a straight answer from her."

"I tell you what I need you to know," Kyler told her.

"Exactly." Telara confronted her. "It all boils down to what you want."

"What I want and what you need are the same," Kyler said simply.

"How do I know that's the truth?" Telara asked while the others watched the exchange between them.

"When you do exactly what I say."

She needs to run for congress with logic like that. Tia's dry comment echoed in their heads.

Telara smirked despite herself. Kyler's scowl deepened.

It looks like the high and mighty crystal keeper can't hear our thoughts. Telara tried to keep her expression neutral, but the smugness was hard to hide.

Good to know. I.Q. chimed in. A chorus of mental agreement followed.

"Are you ready or not?" Kyler's tone sharpened.

We see what you mean. Chance's lips stayed straight, but his head gave the tiniest shake.

With a sigh, Telara stood. "Sure, why not."

Kyler walked to her work bench and grabbed a clear glass bottle that was full of colorful sand. She opened it and put some in the palm of her hand and blew it against the wall with the pictures. As soon as it hit, the pictures all moved away from the swirling circular mass of purples, silvers and black that formed. The same swirling mass Telara saw the last time.

The others looked to Telara, who nodded and said, "That's the portal."

"Enter, and pay attention," Kyler instructed. "What you learn here will determine whether any of this succeeds."

"Yeah, yeah." Telara moved forward while the others followed, she wasn't letting Kyler push her in this time. She paused before she entered the portal and turned to the others. "Just remember, I woke up as my past self when I stepped through."

"As Tien?" Telara nodded at Chad's question. "I can't remember my past name," he turned to the others. "Can you guys?"

I.Q. moved forward behind Telara, "I'll help, let's go."

This time as she moved forward through the portal, she got to see all the colors around her swirling everywhere. When the colors faded and her feet touched the hard ground, she saw that she was in the past Sanctuary like before. The trees with homes in them and trails as well as the big canvas building that took center stage here.

"Whoa." Chad looked down at his clothes, simple woven tunic and boots. "This is too cool."

The others were similarly dressed and visibly changed to reflect their past selves. They tugged at sleeves and collars, amazed by the realism.

A siren blared, silencing the awe.

Tia looked at Telara, "what is that?"

Telara's answer died in her throat as a familiar figure swept in, arm wrapping firmly around her waist.

"Come on, the warning's sounded." Zach said, urging them forward.

"Zach?"

Zach stopped and looked back at her, "is something wrong, Tien?"

"What's going on?" She asked him.

"We'll find out at the main tent," he told her as he continued to urge them forward.

As if anyone will tell us. Cole muttered through their shared link.

Zach halted and turned. "No one's kept anything from us, Zeke. What are you talking about?"

Each of them paused and looked at each other in shock. Telara bit her lips but kept her words to herself. They exchanged furtive glances but kept themselves from speaking via their shared link.

Zach was frowning at them, still waiting for an answer. It was Tia who responded, "Zeke's just having a rough morning." Zach looked unconvinced at her explanation, especially when she stumbled over Zeke's name, so Telara butted in and hoped she could alleviate his confusion.

"With the disappearances and no real answers, it's hard not to question things," she told Zach who sighed and nodded.

His expression softened as he spoke. "You're right. It's been… difficult."

He glanced at Tia. "I'm sorry Chantria, I know not knowing where your father is can't be easy either, but we know they're doing their best to find out."

"Why can't we help?" Vanna asked.

Zach frowned. "They've told us over and over, Jacinta, they worry that we're the actual targets."

"Why?" Chad and Chance both parroted.

At Zach's confused look, Telara figured they might already know this, well their past selves might already know. "Even though we know why, it doesn't mean that it makes sense to us when we really want to help." She told him, which softened his features as he wrapped his arms around her and held her to him.

"I'm sorry Tien, it makes it hard on all of us when we just

want our parents back and to be able to leave this very unforgiving realm with them." He kissed her head. "But we'll do our part and eventually we'll all leave here."

She gave a very indistinct shake of her head when the others looked like they'd question him. "We will," She nodded at Zach. "But for now, let's go find out what's going on." Zach nodded and they all trotted off to the big canvas tent. When they entered the tent, they came to a sudden stop. There, sitting on a bench with Marsella at his side, sat Zane. Zach didn't seem to notice their shock as he moved further into the room. They looked at each other, their faces pale mirrored each other's shock.

"What happened, Zane?" the blue-skinned Plax asked him, his eyes full of sympathy. A shimmer of unease danced just beneath the surface of the room's energy.

Zane looked up at Plax with the same sharp blue eyes they saw in Haven. "My father and I were following a lead on Zo." He looked over at Tia with remorse shining in his eyes. "I'm sorry Chantria, it was a false lead."

"Where's Lucius?" Marsella asked him gently, pushing her hair behind her ear.

Zane gave a slow shake of his head. "I wish I knew. When we arrived at Lapros, or where it used to be, we were ambushed." His head sank into his hands, exhaustion and defeat mingling in the silence.

Shadows? Cole frowned and looked at Telara but when Zach gave him a confused look, he just shook his head.

"Who would dare?" Kala asked, each word emphasized as she spoke, her arms crossed and brow furrowed. Her dark skin glistened while her brilliant sharp blue eyes narrowed.

"Larsa," Zane said, looking tired. "She had a weapon unlike anything I've ever seen." Marsella placed a comforting hand on his shoulder. Zane raised his head, his eyes showing the pain that he was feeling inside.

"Weapon? Did she find the Primordial Key already?" Kali

turned her purple eyes onto her twin sister, worry shining in them.

"I don't think so." Zane shook his head. "If that was the Primordial Key, I don't think either my father or myself would still be here."

"No one knows the exact details of the Primordial Key," Plax pointed out.

Marsella looked up at him. "You're right, but if Larsa ran to this realm to find the missing pieces, we need to assume it's very powerful." The others nodded and Marsella continued, "I wish Serdita and her siblings would've given us more information on this key."

Plax snorted. "Just on the key? How about why we've been here for centuries? Or why the gods in this realm are protecting Larsa and wanting to get rid of us?" He let out a long sigh and looked back at Zane. "What did the weapon look like?"

"It looked like a chakra; blue crystals lined the blade and had a metal curved rod in the center." Zane said, his eyes seemed glazed as he attempted to describe the weapon. "It glowed and suddenly neither of us could move, then everything went dark. When I opened my eyes I found myself alone on the ground. My father was gone, nowhere to be seen."

"She kidnapped Lucius?" They all stiffened at Marsella's question, sending furtive glances at each other but staying silent. Not even speaking in their mind links about this bombshell that Marsella dropped on them, not wanting to make Zach anymore suspicious. They'd discuss this bit of news later. Zach looked at her but she just gave a small shake of her head.

"We'll get Lucius back," Marsella stated, her voice firm. "But for now, we need to rest and regroup before we react."

"I can't rest," Zane protested. "Our friends are missing, my father is missing, and Larsa needs to pay for her crimes."

"We aren't giving up, we just need to regroup right now," Marsella told him. "Your father would say the same thing, you know this."

Zane sighed but he nodded. "You're right, my love." He rose and kissed her softly before he turned to grin at Telara and the others. "My lovely Tien." He moved towards her with his arms open, it took everything in her not to balk at his hug. "I've missed you, and please don't fret, we'll get your grandfather back."

Telara swallowed hard and nodded, not trusting her voice. Thankfully, Zane moved his attention to Zach. "Zachary, I trust you've been making sure my daughter is protected?"

Zach chuckled. "As much as she'll let me." At that, the tension in the room eased, and all within laughed. The Guardians even chuckled.

Zane grasped Zach's shoulder. "Good man." Zane turned to look at the others. "Tonight, we'll feast and rest, just as my lovely wife has suggested."

Marsella moved to stand with Zane and Telara, her arms wrapping around them both. "We will find Larsa, stop her, and bring her to justice." She spoke with purpose.

"And put her back in prison where she belongs." Plax nodded.

"As a family," Zane stated, kissing both Marsella and Telara on their cheeks.

Telara looked back at the other Guardians with an uncertain smile, unsure of how to move forward. Before any of them could say anything, their world tilted around them, colors filled the air and they were once again back in Kyler's white room. Cole leaned back against the nearest wall, "I think I feel ill." He groaned as he put an arm around his stomach.

Chance chuckled, "Thought you enjoyed the thrill rides?"

"I do, but that was nothing like a thrill ride," Cole rumbled.

"What did you discover?" Kyler asked them.

"The Shadow Master is my father?" Telara asked her. "How could that be?"

Kyler frowned, "I know nothing of this Shadow Master you keep asking about. Did you discover what the traitor did to damage the realms?"

"All they spoke about was our past lives being in danger and the Paladins being separated." I.Q. answered, to which Kyler smirked over at Telara.

"It seems bringing your friends here was a better idea than I thought at first." Kyler continued to smirk at Telara who glared back at her. "Open communication is the only way for us to win this war. Do you really want the traitor to win?" She asked her.

"I want to go back to my life before we came to Sanctuary but we don't always get what we want." Telara countered.

Maybe being more open with one another would be a better solution. Vanna suggested via their mind link. *We're running out of options on figuring out how to defeat the Shadow Master and his Magine without losing our lives.*

Do you think Kyler might know about the Magine? I.Q. asked.

Doubtful, she doesn't even know anything about the Shadow Master, Telara nodded in agreement with Tia.

It doesn't hurt to ask. Vanna responded to Telara's irritation.

Telara looked at Kyler, "and what of the Magine?"

Kyler frowned at her, "I know nothing of this Magine, nor do I care. I care about discovering what the traitor did to damage my realms."

"Of course, all about you," Telara glared at Kyler who glared back.

"You should think about what you want," Kyler told her before her vision went dark.

Telara opened her eyes to see that she was back in her room, laying in her bed and staring up at the ceiling. "Still, no answers." With a sigh, she closed her eyes.

13

"POWER BALL?"

They looked at each other then back at Jerry, but it was Chance who spoke this time. "Seriously? This is what you call training?" Chance wasn't usually one to be confrontational, normally he liked to sit back silently and watch before he spoke. It had been years since they used the Power Ball for training, since that first year at Sanctuary. Since then, their training had become reborn in myth and fire, brutal and transformational. And now, it felt as if Jerry was having them do remedial training, as if they couldn't handle anything else.

It had been several days since they discovered that Zane was Telara's father, well her past self's father. They still had a hard time wrapping their heads around the fact that they had two lives, although their past one seemed more like a dream than reality, and now they had to deal with that news. Each day since that night, they went through the motions, but they weren't truly living. Tired of the secrets and lies, it felt like they were walking a tightrope, never sure when, or if, it'd snap beneath them.

I.Q. had spent the evenings after dinner, tapping on the Stargazer, looking up any information he could find on the

Primordial Key they spoke of, but with little luck. While the Stargazer had become easier for him to work since Zane showed them the Prime Rooms back in Haven, the book seemed to take him a bit longer but he was getting it translated. He wasn't sure if this ability had more to do with his powers or just the fact that he was in both of them so much that it had become his second language, whatever this strange language was.

Now, they were in a training chamber in the bowels of Lumenhall, the one they could manipulate to meet their needs. They could create obstacle courses with rivers of lava, fire breathing dragons, a field of jungle vines waiting to wrap them into green cocoons, but instead they felt as if they were standing in their school gym with volleyball nets.

Jerry had told them that he had a training module that he wanted them to try, they weren't sure what to expect, but this wasn't it.

"No," Jerry replied. "I don't call it training, I call it having fun. Something that you seemed to have forgotten how to do."

"How will Power Ball help us defeat the Shadow Master and his Magine?" Telara asked.

"Humor me," Jerry suggested.

"Whatever," Telara levitated the ball to her hand, where it glowed brightly and levitated several inches from her palm. With a thought she sent it flying over the makeshift net that Jerry had installed to separate the entire training room into one big volleyball arena. Chance caught the ball with a burst of water and sent it back over the net to where Tia floated in the air. She caught the ball in midair and bounced it.

"To me!" Cole used heat to levitate himself off the ground.

Tia grinned as she sent the ball flying with a strong gust of wind. Cole caught it in a ball of flame although the force of Tia's gust sent him back several feet. "Hey, play nice!" His flames sent the ball back towards Tia who used a wind tunnel to send the ball right back towards him. Cole grinned as ice formed in front of him, the ball hitting the ice while turning into a ramp that sent the ball running back towards the other side. Vines shot from the ground and slapped the ball to the other side where an electrical bolt curved around the ball to direct it back towards Telara who stopped the ball between her hands. She set it up to spike it back.

I.Q. lunged up with the help of an electricity bolt to catch the ball in midair, with a crack the ball was sent back over the net. Vanna rode a large leaf up; her vines followed to grab the ball and send it back over the net. Chance sent a wet ball back towards Tia who used her wind to set it up for Telara to spike. Cole conjured a fire geyser to send the ball into the air, setting it up for Chance to water spike it. The air around them warmed in so much wet steam, that they almost missed the ball. Tia lowered herself down to the ground where a whirlwind lifted the ball up for Vanna's vine to smack back.

"Good attempt, but not good enough!" Tia smirked and high-fived Vanna.

Cole and Chad both rushed for the ball, their bodies alight with their powers. They collided before they could get to the ball, Chad's ice cooling off Cole's heat. While Cole fell back, Chad only lost his momentum as the heat from Cole melted his ice, and he fell to a knee.

"Hey! Watch out!" Chad rubbed his arm from the contact with Cole. "Stay in your own lane, dude!"

A lightning streak weaved between them to grab the ball and shoot it over the net towards Tia who floated the ball between her hands, a windy cyclone keeping it there. "Did you guys forget what teamwork was?" she asked, shooting the ball back.

Jerry watched them with a grin on his face as they kept sending the Power Ball back over the net. The kids joined him, watching the Guardians playing Power Ball. "Seems like they learned how to play again, gramps." Lillie said with a grin.

Jerry nodded at her, "that they did, Lillie."

Telara watched the others with the ball while she floated several feet off the ground. How long has it been since they just played with their powers? She couldn't remember honestly, but it felt good. Vanna sent the ball straight in the air with one of her roots so Telara moved forward and spiked the ball down with her mind. Her hands didn't touch the ball; she had them open several inches from the ball when she pushed the ball forward with her mind. Chance sent a water geyser that his brother froze which captured the ball in midair.

"Hey!" Chance glared at his brother, "that was mine, dork!"

Chad smirked as he turned the ice post into an ice track that sent the ball rolling in loops until it shot out back over the net. "Not anymore!" Chad watched the ball fly towards Tia who was waiting with a tornado already forming in front of her. "Hey!" He shouted as water formed around his legs that shot him straight in the air.

Tia was ready with a tornado forming, but distracted by Chad's water-blasted launch into the air. Her vortex wasn't fully formed when the ball smacked her in the stomach, launching her back. A massive leaf caught her as she hit the ground.

The glowing ball dimmed, rolling harmlessly across the court until it returned to its milky-white crystal form.

Telara slowly descended to the ground next to Tia. "You okay?" She asked her as she helped her off the leaf that slowly receded into the ground after Tia stood up.

Tia brushed herself off and chuckled, "I'm good," she looked over at Vanna. "Good save, Van."

After hearing that Tia was okay the guys erupted on the other side. "We did it! We scored!"

Telara rolled her eyes but laughed with them. It felt good to laugh.

"Wow, the Guardians didn't forget how to laugh."

They turned around to see Jeff standing there with other Hunters.

"Yeah, but they also cost me twenty bucks," Trevor grumbled as he handed the bill to a grinning Travis who pocketed it.

"You bet on us?" Vanna frowned at him while the rest of the Guardians laughed and shook their heads.

"Hey, man!" Cole and Chad rushed over to slap hands with the Hunters. "Whatcha doing here?"

"Lucy is here to work with Bernie regarding some paperwork that Jerry isn't so fond of, so we decided to tag along." Jeff grinned.

"Good to see you, guys."

"Hey, Big Time!"

They turned to see Big Time heading their way.

"Hey!" He clasped hands as he reached them. Paul and Wes followed Big Time, grinning at the Guardians.

"Miss us?" Wes asked, holding his arms out.

"We haven't really had the time to miss anyone." Telara shrugged, her lips pulled into a wry grin.

Paul nodded in acknowledgment. "I won't ask how you guys have been."

"We appreciate that," Tia gave him a small smile.

"No hitting on my brother," Wes told her as he put himself between Paul and Tia, while Tia frowned at him. "We don't want to make Lucy jealous now."

"What?" Tia looked at him, her brow furrowed. "I'm not hitting on anyone." She protested.

Paul chuckled and shook his head before he shoved Wes out of the way. "Ignore my brother, he's just playing around."

Tia shook her head, "he is just weird."

Wes smirked, "the best kind of weird."

Telara watched as Tia rolled her eyes, she felt a small smile sneak out.

"So, had any luck with the book?" Big Time approached I.Q.

I.Q. nodded, pulling the book from his back pocket, "I've translated over half the book."

Big Time's eyes widened. "Big time!" A big grin broke out. "So, is it a book that Claw would do anything to get his hands on?"

I.Q. nodded, "Definitely."

"Has it been helpful in any other way?" Big Time asked him.

I.Q. sighed. "It talks about the crystals, actually gives some good information regarding them but I'm not sure exactly how helpful it is for us with our situation."

"Could be that it is helpful but you just haven't figured that part out yet." Big Time shrugged.

I.Q. frowned with a thoughtful look on his face, "that could be." He admitted, then grinned. "Maybe I just need to go into reading the book with a new mindset."

"You got it!" Big Time grinned broadly. "So, what have you learned about the crystals?"

I.Q. pursed his lips, tilted his head, then gave Big Time a side look. "Did you know that there's a crystal tier hierarchy?"

Big Time's grin slipped, as his brow furrowed. "You mean like the Parent Crystals, then the Crims?"

I.Q. shook his head. "The book doesn't even mention the Crims."

"No?" Big Time looked down at his Crim, his expression looking thoughtful.

"But it does mention the Parent Crystals." I.Q.'s words had Big Time looking back up. I.Q. nodded. "Except that they're not the top tier, high tier and powerful but not top tier. Crims would be considered mid-tier if they were even noted in this book."

"Hmmm…" Big Time looked down at the book.

I.Q. nodded. "There are four tiers; Primal, Elder, Channeler, and Vital. Parent Crystals fall under Elder while I'd put Crims under Channeler. The book does mention the healer crystals, memory shards, and even the glamour ones. Those are under Vital."

"So, what ones would be considered Primal?" Big Time frowned.

I.Q. looked over at Telara, her Rotary glinting beneath the lights. "I've never heard of the ones that they have listed in the book, but I do have some thoughts."

"Drake! Big Time!" They turned to see Paul and Wes waving towards him. "Come on, bro. We've got to get going before Lucy sends out Henry after us. Last time, the stupid gator cost me a pair of pants." The laughter rang out at that comment. Jerry grinned and turned to walk out with them following him.

"Coming!" Drake shouted back to them, then turned to I.Q. with a grin. "I'd love to sit down and discuss more of the book, we'll have to find some time before we head home." I.Q. nodded in agreement, watching Drake run to catch up to Paul and Wes who were animatedly talking with Travis and Trevor.

"I guess it's time to head back to our rooms," Vanna said with a small sigh. They all nodded and started towards the still open door.

Chance nodded towards the book that I.Q. still held in his hands. "Did you find out anything in the book about the Primordial Key that Zane and Plax spoke about?"

I.Q. gave a shake of his head. "It wasn't mentioned in any of the tiers of the hierarchy."

"What about that Primal tier you were talking about?" Tia asked.

"Nope." I.Q. held the book between both his hands, staring at the worn cover intently. "Though there were three crystals spoken about in the Primal tier that when combined would ascend beyond the tiers."

"Well, don't leave us in suspense, man!" Cole frowned when I.Q. went silent. "What are the three crystals?"

"According to this book, they're the life crystal, soul crystal, and heart crystal." I.Q. looked from the book to the others. "And I doubt those are keys or Crims," he finished wryly.

"Did the book say how to find them?" Tia asked him.

"Nope." The others groaned when I.Q. gave a curt shake of his head. "It's cryptic. Only says each is destined for a specific person. And warns about someone untrustworthy trying to use them."

"What is the warning?" Cole asked, looking up into the bright sun.

"I don't know, I haven't been able to translate that part," I.Q. admitted.

"Whoa!" Chad looked at him with wide eyes. "I didn't think there was anything that you couldn't figure out."

"I didn't say I couldn't figure it out, just that I haven't yet." I.Q. told him defensively.

"So, does anyone think that key is what Kyler is hoping we'll find?" Tia mused.

"With her, I'm not sure if she even knows what she wants us to find." Telara grimaced. "She isn't very open with who she is, why she's here, or what she wants. But then, she expects me to be open with her. I don't understand why she keeps sending us in the past to our past lives that we know nothing about. She could be working with Larsa for all we know." Telara looked over to see Lucy walking with Jerry. They were walking from Lumenhall, but not towards Jerry's place.

"Come on T," Tia said, pulling Telara's attention back to her. "She keeps sending you into the past, then asks you what you discover? You already said that she doesn't seem to care to help us defeat the Shadow Master, something we saw last night as well." They didn't call the Shadow Master Zane, it made it harder on them and after what they learned last night, it was worse. They hadn't even discussed the fact that Zane was Tien's father, and in a way, Telara's. "She's looking for something, but she won't tell you what? What if it is this key? What if the key might be the..." she paused a moment, as if she was attempting to think of a way to say it but then continued with a shrug. "Key to us defeating the Magine without dying?"

"But why?" Telara looked down at the road as they walked, her mind feeling like it was churning but nothing made sense.

"Why what?" Tia frowned.

"Why would she need this key?"

"What do you mean?" I.Q. asked her.

"She's pretty powerful herself. Why would she need us to find it for her? Couldn't she just find it herself?" Telara asked.

"You would think," Vanna's brow furrowed.

"Yeah," Chance spoke slowly. "Something isn't adding up." He agreed. "Maybe we should look into the key, see what it is and what it does. Maybe that will tell us why she wants it and maybe explain why she's having you look for it for her."

"IF that's what she's looking for," Telara reminded him. "It might not have anything to do with why she keeps sending us into the past."

"But it could," I.Q. told her. "We should at least attempt to look into it, better than just doing nothing. Not like she's going to be any forthcoming, right?"

"No, she won't," Telara groaned.

"This is aggravating," Tia sighed.

"At least this time I didn't have to tell you about what happened, you were there," Telara said with a small smile. "It feels a lot better, honestly." The others chuckled at that, they understood how she felt. They all felt this was a lot better.

14

Lucius watched the Guardians through the vision portal that he created. He wanted to keep an eye on the Guardians, but on his terms, not something controlled by Hades. He watched as they walked back to Jerry's home and sighed.

"I'm sorry," he murmured, eyes locked on the portal as a surge of helplessness rose in his chest. He hated being trapped in this stone prison while the others fought, while they lived.

"I've handled everything so badly."

"About time you admitted your fault in all this."

Lucius turned at the soft, feminine voice. A lovely goddess stood before him, her presence commanding but strangely muted. She wore a white cotton tunic with greyed edges; a heavy wool cloak draped over her shoulders. The cloak aged her, but the silver laurel on her head and matching adornments hinted at vitality, though none reached her eyes. Her gaze held the weight of many years.

"Persephone?" he asked, brow furrowed.

She nodded, her tone quiet but precise. "Very good. You're quite knowledgeable. Perhaps a bit too trusting though."

"I've been told that before," Lucius admitted, watching

her warily. He had never met the wife of Hades, but from what he'd heard, he expected someone youthful and vibrant. This woman was neither. Her complexion was flawless but tinged with a cold, gray hue. Her expression was neutral, even unreadable. She reminded him of the very few deities capable of true stoicism. Most wore their emotions like armor.

"What are you doing here?" He asked bluntly. He asked her, knowing that gods and goddesses could beat around the bush for hours and even longer if they chose. He chose to cut to the chase, he didn't feel like playing cat and mouse with her.

"My husband is in turmoil," she replied, as though that explained everything.

Lucius glanced toward the portal, where he saw the Guardians return to Jerry and Lin's.

"He's not the only one."

"He's the only one that matters to me." Her voice remained calm. "You made a promise to my husband, a promise you broke."

"A promise I was forced into," Lucius said sharply. "And one Hades knew I couldn't keep once my family returned. It was a vow that never should've been asked of me."

"Yet you made it," she said, her chin lifting slightly. "And your decision has caused my husband pain."

"No," Lucius countered, his tone cold. "The fact that he's trying to protect a daughter he had with another woman is what's tearing him apart. And in doing so, he's damned my family, and hasn't given them a second thought."

The corners of her eyes tightened, just slightly, but she said nothing to confirm the sting of his words.

"My husband may have made questionable choices," she said at last, "but they were made with the best intentions. Can you say the same?"

"Yes. I can." Lucius crossed his arms, unmoved. "What I

find interesting is that you don't seem all that jealous about your husband's child with another woman. Why is that?"

"I never said I wasn't jealous." Persephone replied.

"So, you *are* jealous," he said, eyes narrowing as he studied her face. He watched her carefully, piecing things together.

"Of course, I was jealous," Persephone admitted, her hands now folded gently in front of her. "It is the way of the gods. Look at Hera and Zeus. She's endured countless betrayals."

"Yes," Lucius said bitterly, "and it's always the innocent who suffer the consequences. But in this case, you couldn't punish the mother, could you? She was returned to her realm too quickly."

"Innocent?" Persephone scoffed. "They would be with one they knew to be tied to another, they brought their own misfortunes upon themselves."

"Not always," Lucius countered. "How many times did the gods disguise themselves? How is that their fault?"

Penelope shrugged. "That isn't my concern."

"Then what is?" Lucius watched her.

Persephone tilted her head at him, then shrugged lightly. "I want my husband to be happy."

With those words, she turned and walked only a few steps before vanishing from sight.

Lucius stared at the empty space where she'd stood, then made his way back to the stone bench. Settling onto it, he looked once more into the portal. A wry grin pulled at his lips.

"Well, granddaughter," he murmured, "you'd be truly amused to see me now. I feel the same aggravation I used to see in your eyes so many times. What I wouldn't give for a do-over."

~

"Jeff!" They turned to see Stazi glaring at Jeff, both were standing by hole thirteen that was situated in the middle of Arcadia, close to the pond. Stazi was brandishing her golf club in a menacing manner while Jeff was rolling on the ground laughing. His laughter echoed all around them. They looked at each other, all confused at what they were seeing. "You can't lift your ball without marking it, and you don't get to put your ball back closer to the hole!"

Jeff sat up, still laughing and attempting to reply through his laughter. "Sure I can, I just did it." He pointed to where his ball lay, only inches from the hole. He was still laughing when Stazi walked over to his ball, picked it up, and threw it into the pond.

"Try to get out of that!" She told him, her glare deepening when all he did was laugh even harder. "Keep this up and you'll be wearing an authentic golf club bow tie!" She pointed her club at him.

Jeff rose from the ground, his face still showing amusement. "Fine, fine. You're no fun." They watched him walk over to the pond where an alligator emerged with the ball in his mouth. "Thanks, Clifford." They heard Jeff say before walking back to Stazi.

"First Henry and now Clifford?" Cole looked at them. They just shrugged their shoulders and continued walking. Several weeks had passed since their Power Ball game when they got to see their friends from Alaska. Their days were spent walking around Arcadia, meeting some of the residents here, and working on their powers in an empty field they found by a dog park or down in the basement of Lumenhall. Although in the empty field they found some power lines there where I.Q. discovered he could pull electricity from the lines. Today was a day they had decided to do a walkabout, as many of the locals here call walking around Arcadia.

"Move it!"

They turned at the shout and all leapt to the side as two

elderly women raced their wheelchairs by them. They were laughing and hollering for everyone to get out of their way as they continued down the road. Jenna and Patty were racing each other through the streets on their wheelchairs, something that might be odd at normal retirement homes, but not this one. They watched as many moved out of the way without breaking stride in their movements or conversations This wasn't the first time they had seen this, although this was the first time they had been almost run over. As they watched, Jenna and Patty raced by Lucy who was walking with Jayne. They both cheered the two racers on as they sped by.

Cole looked at the others. "Did you just see that?"

Vanna frowned at him, "Not the first time we 've seen Jenna and Patty racing."

"No," Cole frowned at her. "Lucy and Jayne, they're cheering them on." He gave them an expectant stare with his head tilted slightly, waiting for the realization to come to them. When they all shrugged their shoulders, he continued, "Why isn't Lucy lecturing them on breaking the rules? She gets on everyone for breaking the rules, and the kids told us that there isn't supposed to be any racing in the streets. They even said the two are breaking the rules."

Chance had already pushed himself up and was brushing grass and dirt off his clothes. "You want to go ask her, be my guest."

"I'll pass." Cole was already standing, shaking his head. "She doesn't seem to like me very much."

"Probably because you like to break the rules and mess up her paperwork," Tia pointed out with a smirk.

"Whatever." Cole grumbled as they continued their walkabout.

"Does anyone know the definition of walkabout?" I.Q. mused as they walked.

"Isn't it something to do with Australia?" Chad asked.

I.Q. nodded, "that is one definition, a journey taken by an Australian Aboriginal on foot. I was thinking of the British term."

"British?" Chance's brow wrinkled. "They use that term as well?"

Another nod from I.Q. before he answered, "yes, they consider it an informal stroll among a crowd conducted by an important visitor."

"Like the queen or king." Vanna supplied.

"Yup." I.Q. responded.

"You want to be the one to tell the little dictators?" Cole asked him with a smirk.

I.Q. shrugged, "it can also mean to wander in a leisurely way."

Cole snorted. "Sounds like a cop out to me."

I.Q. shrugged, "prove me wrong." The others laughed, I.Q. had always been the smartest one in the group. Although the past few years it hasn't truly shown that, everything they were dealing with had been completely new to all of them. He had to basically put aside all that he knew and learn to accept the myths he once believed to be unrealistic, as now facts.

"Airmail!"

As they neared the clubhouse, they heard the familiar voice shouting from over near the tennis courts. They turned to see Wes, Paul, Travis and James playing cornhole right next to the tennis courts. James was grinning broadly while Travis was nodding with a smug look.

"Cancel him out, Pauly!" Wes shouted.

They watched the four playing until Wes shouted out, "21 wins it!" He and Paul exchanged a quick fist bump before turning to Travis and James, who reluctantly returned it with matching grimaces.

"Yeah, well the old men just have too much time on their hands," James grinned and leapt back from Paul.

They kept moving forward, leaving the four guys back there joshing with each other. They stopped when they saw Trevor by another one of the ponds that were situated around Arcadia. Trevor was skipping rocks with Stella, the Alpha weapons expert from Sanctuary and Joe, one of the Beta warriors from Sanctuary. Upon seeing them, Trevor handed over his rocks to Stella and trotted over to them. "Hey guys."

"Hi!" They smiled at him.

"Why aren't you playing cornhole?" Chance asked him.

Trevor shook his head, "no way! Wes and Paul play professionally. It isn't as much fun when you know you won't win."

"What about just having fun?" Vanna suggested. "It isn't all about winning."

"Then why keep score if it isn't all about winning?" Trevor shot back. "Exactly." He said when Vanna just frowned at him, with a wink he turned and headed back to Stella and Joe.

"Billy, you're dead meat!"

They turned to see Lucy running after Billy who was running ahead of her and laughing. In his hands was the tablet that they saw Lucy carrying around with her earlier.

"If you damage my pad, I'll shave your head!" She threatened.

Billie, Billy's twin sister, stood there with Jayne while Lucy threatened Billy. They both were grinning although when Lucy threatened to shave Billy's mohawk off, his sister's eyes widened. They looked at each other. "Is everyone here?" Vanna asked, looking around them at all their friends from Sanctuary, Alaska, Citadel, and even Haven.

"Why haven't they approached us?" Telara wondered as they realized exactly how many of them were there.

"Not like you've been very approachable."

They turned to see Gage leaning against a tree about five feet away from them.

Telara swallowed hard, normally she'd give him grief for

sneaking up on them, but he was right. "Sorry." She said softly.

Gage shrugged. "We know you've been through a lot." He spoke.

"That's an understatement," Telara muttered.

"But," Gage continued. "So have we. Pam is our friend as well, many of us have not only known her longer, some of us better than others." He looked over at one of the many pavilions in Arcadia, where they saw Tobias, Zeke and Claw talking animatedly. They knew there were many at Sanctuary that had close relationships to Pam, though they wouldn't put Claw in that category, but everyone had been hurt by her departure.

Telara nodded to Gage, he was right.

We didn't think about their feelings. Chance grimaced and looked away. When speaking through their mind link, they have learned to look away from each other so that their silent communication wasn't so obvious.

We let our pain override everything. Tia agreed.

Telara breathed in deeply before she responded. "We're sorry, Gage. I guess we've been so engrossed in our own sorrows that we forgot that we weren't the only ones hurt by Pam's decision." She pressed her lips together, then she looked up at Gage, leery about what she'd see in his face.

A smile was definitely not what she thought she'd see. "Tell you what," Gage told them. "You can make it up to us by playing a round of rainbow ball."

"Rainbow ball?" Cole frowned. "You want us to go back to Sanctuary?"

Gage laughed, "no, haven't you guys been to Hallowmere Door?" He asked them.

Telara frowned and gave a shake of her head, "Not really, not much time to play, mostly what we've done in Lumenhall is train."

"Well, we did play Power Ball," Cole interjected.

"Only because Jerry insisted," Chance said.

Gage laughed, "I can see that. Come on." He told them with a wave, moving towards the clubhouse. "You need to see more of Lumenhall and especially Hallowmere Door."

They shrugged and followed him to Lumenhall. Through the normal doors of the clubhouse for outsiders to see and down through the staircase into the deep reaches below that was Lumenhall. They followed him going the opposite way of the training area, the only area they truly explored here. They passed the archives where he told them that Zeke would always sneak off to, and where they'd have to go drag him out many hours later.

They came to an arched slab of stone, nothing spectacular, rather boring. They looked around them when Gage stopped and turned with a grin.

Chance looked around and frowned. "Thought we were going to Hallowmere Door?" he asked.

Gage nodded. "We are." They frowned at him, then gasped when he placed his hand on the stone slab. As soon as his hand touched the stone, it lit up. Soft silver runes began to shimmer across the surface like ripples on still water. A slender line of light traces the outline of the arch, glowing brighter with each rune it touched until there was a complete arch of lit up runes. In the center of the stone arched slab, a tree started to form, separating the stone slab and creating an opening. The tree glowed and moved back into the room, until it settled behind the bar.

They moved through the opening, their eyes wide as they stared around them in amazement. The ceiling arched high above, seeing floating lanterns up there that drifted like fire-flies. Long wooden tables stretched across the room; mismatched chairs filled with many they recognized and some they didn't. Humans and supernatural creatures of all sorts, dryads, dwarves, and many others. Hallowmere dwarfed Czaar's Cantina by a lot.

At the back of Hallowmere they saw a great hearth that burned at the far end, its flame a gentle violet, but cast no smoke they could see. The walls were carved stone, draped with ivy and glowing with slow-moving balls of light that moved around the room slowly. Soft music from unseen instruments, and the air was thick with laughter and chatter.

"Hey Gage!" A man who looked as if he was carved from stone walked up to Gage and grasped his hand in a friendly shake.

"Vasel!" Gage grinned and clasped his shoulder with his free hand. He then turned to them. "I want you to meet the Guardians. Telara, Tia, Cole, Chance, Vanna, I.Q. and Chad." They nodded to him as Gage spoke their names one by one.

"I've heard you were in Arcadia," Vasel told them. "Jerry wasn't sure when you'd eventually meander down this way. I told him sooner or later you'd want to put your feet up and let your cares sail down the river of Hallowmere." He winked at them.

"River of Hallowmere?" Chance frowned and looked around them.

Vasel laughed. "There is a river that runs beneath us that I like to call the river of Hallowmere, although Jerry swears it is the Merano river." Vasel shrugged. "So, we agree to disagree. Have fun and enjoy, I need to get back behind the bar before Tuck robs me blind."

They looked at Gage with a frown, but he just grinned. "Tuck is an imp, a very mischievous one who likes shiny things." They all nodded in understanding.

"Rainbow Ball!" Cole and Chad rushed to the table where two Arions had just finished a game and were ambling away to a table.

"Let them have fun," Gage said when it seemed they were about to stop the boys. "Let's go visit, you have Sanctuary, Alaska, Citadel, and there are even some Havenites here."

"Havenites?" Tia frowned.

"The ones from Haven," Gage told them.

"Since when were they called Havenites?" Telara looked at him as they followed him over to a table closest to the wall by the hearth. There was a long wooden bench with green pillows for comfort. As they took their seats Travis and James joined them while Paul and Wes were watching Cole and Chad. Chance chuckled when he saw Paul and Wes start taking bets on the game.

"If you believed everything he said, you'd believe that he can defeat the Shadow Master himself," Travis snorted. They turned to listen to him and James as they spoke.

"With one hand behind his back," James added wryly, the others chuckled at that.

"Who are you talking about?" Chance asked them.

"Stan the man," Trevor said with an eye roll.

"Stan the man?" Vanna frowned.

"That is what he calls himself." Travis snorted. "I call him utterly useless."

"Him and Larry both," James interjected.

"If you don't believe us, you can ask Lucy." Jeff smirked as he entered the room and pulled a chair out for himself. "Those two irritate her to no end." He smirked. "About the only good thing about those two."

Vanna frowned at him. "Why is Stan and Larry irritating Lucy a good thing?"

"Because if she's getting on them then she's leaving me alone," Jeff smirked and the others laughed and nodded in agreement.

Cole chuckled and looked over at Vanna. "I can see where they're coming from, Lucy seems a bit uptight to me, I'd rather see her yelling at someone other than me too."

Tia rolled her eyes, "That is because you never do what you're supposed to."

The Hunters laughed at her remark, Travis fist bumping Cole

Telara turned to Gage. "Are you visiting family?" She liked the idea of meeting his family. Ever since they came to Sanctuary, it had been hard to picture anyone they'd met with something as ordinary as a family. It made them feel more… human, somehow. Like maybe they were just regular people, too.

"Not really," he admitted.

"Whatcha doing here, then?" She asked, then sighed at his raised brow. "I don't mean any disrespect, I swear, I'm just curious. I'd actually like to meet your family." She admitted.

"I'm here to help," he told her.

She frowned, "what do you mean, to help?" She asked him.

"You're not going to fight alone." He told her and she felt her body go cold at hearing that.

"No!" She shouted and jumped up.

"Telara!" Tia rose and moved towards her.

"No, Tia," Telara told her, feeling tears well up inside. "I won't lose any more friends; I want to see them and talk to them but they aren't joining us in this fight." She looked at Gage, then at everyone who was watching her warily. "No! You guys aren't fighting!" With those words she turned and rushed out of Hallowmere with the other Guardians running after her.

15

"Time to wake up."

Telara's eyes snapped open and she jerked up to notice that she was no longer in her room. She looked down at the padded lounge chair she was now sitting on, looking around her she saw that the walls had an earthen feel as if this room was built inside a tree or underground. It took her a moment to realize what actually woke her up, that voice. She turned and there he stood.

"Zach?" She asked and when he nodded, she leapt up and hugged him close. "Where have you been?"

He held her to him and spoke into her hair, "I've been unable to reach you until now, I kept trying but couldn't find you. It felt as if I was stuck in limbo."

She moved back and smacked his chest. "You should've tried harder." She shrugged and laughed when he raised a brow. "I'm just glad to see you."

"I'm glad to see you too."

"Hey T! You here?"

Her eyes widened as she looked at Zach. "Is that Chance?" He nodded and they moved to go outside where the others stood, all looking like they did the last time they went into their past. She looked at Zach. "What's going on?"

"Does he know who we are?" Cole asked her.

"Yes, I do, brother." Zach told him. Cole frowned at him when he called him brother. "I remember everything now."

"I think you need to explain that," Telara told him.

Zach turned and grinned at her, "my lovely Tien, as smart, beautiful and mouthy as ever. I've missed you."

Telara's brow furrowed at his words, although from her trips into the past, she knew that they were close; and, from the first time, she felt something between them. "So, can you tell us what happened?" she asked him.

"I wish I could," he told her with a wry grin. "We were in Sanctuary and when we learned that your grandfather was being held by Hades, we went to Tartarus to save him. We were ambushed by the demons of the underworld, then nothing."

"Nothing?" Telara frowned at him.

"We were fighting the demons but then there was nothing but darkness," Zach admitted. "I would awaken and try to talk to previous Guardians but they never heard me, until you." He smiled at Telara. "I knew you needed me and that I needed to help you."

"Why didn't you tell me about all this before?" Telara demanded.

"I couldn't," he admitted. "I couldn't remember anything except that I needed to help you, things would come to me in patches but I couldn't remember everything, no matter how hard I tried."

"And now you can?" I.Q. queried.

Zach nodded. "Whatever kept my memory from me, started to slowly fade away over a year ago."

"Why didn't you reach out to me then?" Telara asked him.

"I tried but it seemed as if your mind was closed to me," he told her.

"But now it's not?" She asked him and he shook his head. "I wonder why?" She mused.

"Could it be Kyler, do you think?" Tia asked.

Telara looked at Zach, "did Kyler free you?"

"I don't know who this Kyler is," he admitted. "I never knew what it was that wouldn't let me speak of the past."

They looked around them, then back to Zach. "So, why did you bring us here?" Telara asked him. "This is where Kyler always sends us when she sends us into the past."

Zach looked around them, then shrugged. "I didn't bring us here; I was looking for you and this is where I came. I thought you brought us here." He told her.

"Maybe Kyler's trips to the past have something to do with Zach's memories?" I.Q. suggested looking around as the others nodded.

"Sounds plausible to me." Vanna shrugged.

"So, what do we do now?" Chad asked. "What are we here for?"

"You're here to heal." They turned at the childish voice they heard from behind. There stood a little boy around ten years old.

"Who are you?" Chance asked him.

"Nikos." Zach said with a grin. "Hey pal, are you truly here?"

"Are any of us truly here?" Nikos asked them, his brown hair falling over his eyes. He raised a small hand to brush that hair from over his eyes, and pushed it behind his ear.

"What do you mean by that?" Telara frowned at him, curious as to how Zach knew him but not liking how vague he sounded. She was tired of not getting answers.

"This is a dream, is it not?" Nikos stared right at Telara, his brown eyes seemed too old for his childish body.

"I guess..." Telara watched him closely. "What do you know?" she asked him. "And don't say, what do any of us know," she told him, hands on her hips, staring at him.

Nikos gave a mischievous grin. "Okay, I won't."

She frowned when he said nothing. "Look, kid, we're tired of games."

"But games are fun," he said with the precocious manner of a child.

She looked back at Zach who shrugged his shoulders. When she turned back to Nikos, he was gone. "What the-?" She turned to look at the others but they were gone as well. "What's going on?" She looked around.

"Hello, Tien."

She froze hearing that voice, with slow precision she turned and standing there was Zane. She frowned at him. "What're you doing here?"

"Just wondering if you were ready to talk yet." He watched her.

"Why didn't you tell me that you're the father to my past self?" she asked him.

"I didn't tell you that I'm your father because I didn't think you were ready," he told her. "Although, I'm glad that you know."

"Not my father," she corrected him. "My past self. I have a father who has always been there for me, but thanks to you and your stupid Magine, I lost him."

He shook his head. "You and your past self are one and the same, Tien. You keep denying that and you keep denying your true self."

"What's that supposed to mean?" she demanded.

He moved closer to her but she stepped back shaking her head, so he stayed where he was with a sigh. "The reason you can't truly embrace your powers is that you can't embrace yourself, your true self. Tien, the daughter of Zane and Marsella. A past Guardian with so much power, that the gods were intimidated. The gods don't want you to regain your power or your memories because then they'd have no control over you. They took Lucius because they feared he'd finally tell you everything."

"What does it matter if someone tells us everything? If we can't remember it, what does it matter?" she practically screamed at him. "We don't know what everyone wants from us. We don't know what's expected of us except to die at the hands of your Magine."

Zane moved so swift, she didn't see him until he stood right in front of her. He reached out and held her arms in his grip, his intense gaze meeting hers. "Who cares what everyone wants? What do you want?" he asked her.

"What do I want?" she asked him, her eyes full of tears and her body shaking. "I want to wake up from this nightmare back in my bed in Michigan. I want to wake up with my family and I want all this to be nothing more than a bad dream. That's what I want!" She told him, her voice breaking.

Zane stared at her, his eyes full of pain at her words. When he spoke, his voice was raspy with emotion. "I'm sorry that you're going through this, Tien. But I want you to know I love you and only want you to be happy." With those words, the world around her started to fade away, until there was only darkness.

"Telara!"

She opened her eyes to see Tia above her, staring down at her in her room in Arcadia. She sighed.

"Hey, what happened?" Tia asked her. "We were there with you and Zach and suddenly we woke up in our rooms but when we came in here you were still sleeping."

"Zane decided he wanted a father/daughter chat." She grimaced, then groaned. "I need to learn how to control my dreams so other people can quit hijacking them."

"Naughty Shadows … Evil Shadows … great big blobs of doom!"

"Controlled Shadows … Scary Shadows … Gloom! Gloom! Gloom!"

Pam's eyes narrowed at the smaller Shadows prancing around like children in a schoolyard play, their eerie chant bouncing off the stone walls. She bit back a smirk when Bac got a well-earned swat from Kele after trying to trip Knucker. Those three were always at it. Strange little things, playful in a way that made them feel almost harmless. Almost. Unlike their hulking counterparts, they didn't snarl or tower, didn't obey commands or bow to any hierarchy. They were chaos wrapped in shadows. But entertaining.

"You forget, after a while," came a calm, velvety voice behind her. "That they used to terrify you."

Pam turned to see the pale woman standing there, her lips forming a slight smile as she watched the mini shadows dancing and singing.

"I don't know if terrified is the word I'd use," Pam replied, eyes sliding back to the vanishing Shadows. "I fought them. And won. More than once."

The woman gave a slow, almost indulgent nod. "You can fight something and still be afraid of it. Fear and victory are not mutually exclusive."

Pam turned from the woman and watched the mini shadows, who disappeared around a corner, saying nothing.

"You keep to yourself," the woman observed. "Most people who end up here tend to cling to others. Misery loves company. But you…" She trailed off, her gaze sharpening. "You're different."

"I'm not most people." Pam shrugged.

The woman gave a shake of her head. "No, you definitely are not." She agreed.

"Look, I have my own reasons for being here."

"Your brother," the woman said smoothly.

Pam stiffened, just slightly, but it was enough.

The woman's laugh was quiet and wry. "Oh, the things we do for family. Sacrifice. Scheme. Endure."

Pam studied her carefully. "Do they ever appreciate it?"

The woman's expression shifted, something old and bitter flickered behind her pale features. "Rarely," she said softly. "They don't see the price we pay. Not really."

Pam didn't respond right away. The silence between them stretched, filled only by the faint sounds of far-off laughter and the ever-present hum of shadow energy in the walls.

"If you ever find yourself wanting someone to talk to..." The woman's tone shifted again, all silk and shadow. "You're welcome in my room. It's the last one on the upper floor. Opposite Zane's." She smiled, that same unreadable curve of her lips, and turned to leave.

Pam watched her go, her brow furrowed. A parting gift, an invitation or a warning, she couldn't be sure. Either way, the game was on.

"BE CAREFUL PAM." LUCIUS SOFTLY SPOKE AS HE WATCHED THE small portal in his cell. He was thankful for that portal so that he had an eye into the outside world but it also frustrated him that he could do nothing for his friends out there. As much as he tried not to conjure the portal, in case Hades was watching and enjoying his discomfort, he also worried about everyone and needed to check in on them. "You can't trust that woman, she lies and will do anything to further her own agenda."

"I thought you said she was your mother." Hades appeared outside his cell with a scowl on his face.

"I did." Lucius stared at him. "I guess that makes you, my grandpa." The tone Lucius spoke with showed how unenthused he was with that little bit of knowledge.

Hades' scowl darkened at his words. "I want nothing to

do with a boy who doesn't even show his mother any respect."

"How can I respect someone who killed the woman I love? Whose only goal is to enslave our entire realm to her wishes." He countered.

"You lie!" Hades screamed at him. "She would never do such things; she's the spitting image of her mother."

"I wouldn't know, my grandmother passed away before I was born at the hands of her daughter."

Hades erupted into a flame of pure anger that heated the cavern up, so much was the flames that Lucius had to shield his eyes with his hand.

Lucius sighed and turned back to the portal where he watched Pam turn down another hallway. "Be careful." He told her silently.

16

TELARA LOOKED out over the pond while she sat on a nearby bench. A noise to her right caught her attention. She grinned when she saw Henry settle on the grass next to the bench. She chuckled to herself. Before meeting Jerry, she would've freaked out over seeing a gator crawling up next to her. Now, it just felt like a normal day here at The Hills. I.Q. was playing golf with Jerry. Cole and Chad were attempting to beat Wes and Paul at the cornhole, with little success, while the others watched and cheered.

She told the others about her conversation with Zane in the morning, but other than that, they hadn't spoken about their dreams. She felt thankful that the others were there for most of the dream. That way she didn't have to repeat everything. They were all trying to process everything that has happened and their feelings regarding it. Her resolve to stay unemotional and distant from others, wasn't as strong as before.

She needed some time to herself so she found a quiet place. She didn't mind that Henry joined. She moved rocks around the pond with her mind while she sat there. Creating multiple rock structures around the pond when she heard a whispered, "impressive." She let the rock that she had been levitating fall into the pond with a plop.

She turned to see Lin standing there with Bear in her arms. She gave a small smile that didn't quite reach her eyes as she turned back to moving rocks around. "Not really, these are really basic moves, nothing spectacular."

"To those without power, it is pretty spectacular," Lin continued. She moved closer to the bench, "May I join you?" She asked and when Telara nodded she sat down but stayed silent.

After a few moments Telara spoke, "growing up as a kid, I used to think it'd be cool to get powers." She grimaced, "then we got them."

"And a whole lot of baggage." Lin responded.

Telara nodded, "yeah."

"It's a lot for anyone to handle, especially when you don't get time to process it."

Telara's head leaned back as she stared into the sky, "the time wouldn't be so bad if we would've gotten all the info."

"You sure about that?" Lin asked her.

"No," Telara sighed. "I'm not. As soon as we feel as if we're starting to process everything, something else happens. When we feel on solid ground," Telara paused, trying to think how to put her thoughts into words.

"The floor disappears from beneath your feet." Lin supplied and she nodded.

"Every move we make, we question everything. We second guess ourselves." Telara looked back at the pond. "We question everything. Will this backfire on us? Is this what we're supposed to do? What if we mess up?" Telara groaned. "It's too overwhelming.'

"Only if you let it be."

Telara looked back at Lin. "What do you mean?"

"Life is only as bad or good as you let it be."

Telara shot Lin a sardonic look.

Lin smiled at her. "I'm serious. Are you going to deal with more betrayal? I'm sure you will."

"You're not much help," Telara retorted.

"I'm sure I've heard you say that you wanted people to stop lying to you, I'm just telling you the truth." Lin patted her hand.

Telara sighed. "You're right."

Lin stood up with Bear in her arms and left Telara with this parting shot. "You can either wallow in self-pity or you can play the hand you've been dealt on your terms. Your choice."

Telara didn't watch Lin leave, rather she stared into the watery surface of the pond and pondered what Lin had told her.

"I THINK I KINDA LIKE HAVING A BROTHER," COLE MUSED AS they walked back towards Jerry and Lin's home. Telara had been musing silently over her conversation with Lin, while Cole and Chad had been arguing over whose fault it was that they lost the cornhole match. So, when he said that, somewhat out of the blue, she almost tripped over her feet.

"Hey!" Chance caught her and helped steady her. "Don't worry, the floor breaks everyone eventually," he told her when she looked up at him, making her smile.

"Thanks," she murmured, brushing her hair behind her ear.

"And they said ballet wasn't your calling." Cole smirked at her.

She raised a brow at his words and shot back, "Not as smooth as your brother."

He shrugged. "We'll blame that on him."

"How?" Vanna looked at him.

"He wasn't around." Cole smirked. "If he had been reborn with me, maybe he could've helped with that."

"I'd like to know why he didn't," I.Q. spoke with the others nodding in agreement.

"I'd like to know how we died," Tia grumbled.

Vanna stopped in mid-stride and turned to stare at Tia. "Seriously?" she asked.

Tia nodded. "Might explain why the leaders want us to just run to our deaths without asking questions."

"What do you mean?" Telara asked her.

"What if they were involved in our deaths?" Tia said softly. "And what if digging deeper proves they're the ones responsible?"

"And… finding out the answer just might save us." Chance interjected, then shot a wary look Telara's way.

Telara nodded and laughed at the expressions staring back at her. "Considering everything we've figured out, Pam or no Pam, I'm over marching toward doom without asking why. I want real answers."

"Yes!" Chance leapt skyward, fist raised high like a runner crossing the finish line, eyes shining with wild excitement. When the others gave him a funny look, he grinned sheepishly. "I missed the old Telara." The others nodded with him.

"Seeing my bro was an inspiration, huh?" Cole smirked, but Telara just rolled her eyes.

"Was there anything in the Stargazer about our deaths?" Tia turned to I.Q. and asked.

I.Q. gave a shake of his head. "Unfortunately, no. Mostly it truly reads like a diary. Lucius wrote about his life growing up in his realm, how he believes that his mother killed his grandmother and father." He stopped and nodded when the others gasped. "I know. It reads almost word for word the plays we saw in Haven. There are some minor changes and parts that weren't shown in the plays."

"What parts weren't included in the play?" Chad asked him.

"The Stargazer spoke of Lucius growing up in a palace with a mother who only cared about power, she hated him, hated that he looked so much like his father. Another man she hated."

"Really?" Telara started to feel for Lucius, her grandfather, as I.Q. gave a nod and grimace.

"It details their journey to Earth and how they set up Sanctuary." I.Q. continued.

"Cool." Chance's eyes lit up.

"Also talks about us growing up there and how suddenly it felt as if the gods had turned against us all." I.Q. shrugged. "Only problem is there was no proof."

"So… maybe our deaths are the proof?" Tia suggested while the others frowned, except for I.Q. whose expression went from pensive to epiphanic.

"We discover how we died, we could uncover everything." I.Q. spoke slowly.

"Do you think that's what Kyler is wanting us to find out?" Vanna looked at Telara, who was silently mulling over all that was being said.

Telara looked up, her expression thoughtful and perplexed. "Do we really think our deaths are the key to finding out what happened and who was behind it?"

Tia grinned at her. "You got a better explanation?"

Telara shook her head and looked at each of them with a grin. "Let's find out how we died, shall we?"

I.Q. opened his mouth to say something but a shrill alarm sounded that drowned out whatever he was about to say.

"What the-?" Telara frowned looking around.

"Hey, Travis, James, Trevor!" Cole shouted at the Hunters as they ran up to them.

"What's going on?" Chad asked them as they approached.

"Flint has been spotted." Trevor paused and told them as Travis and James kept running past with a jaunty wave.

"What about Pam?" Telara asked him.

Trevor shrugged.

"You guys want our help?" Cole asked, pulling his necklace from around his neck.

"Nah!" Trevor waved at him. "Just keep your eyes open, we aren't even sure where he is, just that he's been spotted so we're going to start canvassing in that area."

"Come on Sally, quit flirting and let's get to work." Travis shouted back.

"Both you Sallys need to hurry up, or else I'll take care of this all on my own." James shouted back as he followed the road that veered towards the left. Trevor waved at them and took off, attempting to catch up to both Travis and James.

Telara gave a shrug. "Oh well, I'd rather work on the Stargazer than have to deal with Flint anyways."

"I'm hurt; I thought we had made a connection."

They turned and saw Flint standing there next to one of the lampposts, leaning against it.

"Flint!" Cole glared at him.

Telara folded her arms while glaring at him. "What're you doing here?"

"Just wanted to talk," he told her. She gave him a sardonic look. "Or won't your handlers let you?" He asked her.

Tia snorted. "We don't have handlers, that's what you and your sister have."

Flint looked at her and grinned. "If you want to believe that, then go ahead."

"What do you want?"

"Pam misses you." He told them simply.

"Then she shouldn't have left."

"She is trying to help you." He countered.

Telara snorted, "yeah, her running to the side that wants us dead is really helping us."

Flint straightened up with eyes flashing. "We don't want you dead!" He denied.

Telara opened her mouth to say something but whatever she was about to say was drowned out by a deafening explosion that shook the ground. They looked around them as the sirens from earlier grew in volume and a voice echoed around them.

"Shadows attacking! West end by hole eight!"

Telara turned to glare at Flint. "You distracted us!"

Flint held up his hands and shook his head. "No, seriously, I had nothing to do with this."

"Yeah, right, like we'd ever believe you."

Flint shook his head, "Whatever, I didn't, but since you won't believe me." He disappeared in a black smoke. They looked at one another and gave frustrated groans.

"We better go and see what's happening." Telara grumbled.

17

"Let's go!" They grabbed their Crims and with a slight touch were geared up. They rushed towards the left side where they could already see smoke rising and people rushing to protect the Hills from the Shadows. Tia let her winds lift her off the ground and guide her forward while Vanna rode a giant leaf with I.Q. and Chance crouching next to her. Cole used his heat to fly next to Vanna while Chad rode his ice track. Telara started to rise off the ground and join them when all around her black smoke started to form, closing off her vision so that she couldn't see anything. She landed back on the ground, not wanting to run into anything and brought up her shield as she looked around her and waited for the attack.

"You have no need to fear, I'm not here to hurt you," a soft feminine voice came from the smoke but Telara could still not see anyone. The voice sounded familiar.

"If I've no reason to fear you, why don't you show yourself? Or are you afraid?" Telara challenged, hands at the ready in case of an attack.

A movement from her right had her turn to see a figure emerge from the shadows. A cloaked figure that was reminiscent of the battle in Alaska. "You!" Telara frowned, jumping back to where she hung in the air several feet from the ground, her rotary glowing.

The figure lifted the gaunt, pale fingers to pull back the hood and reveal herself. Her skin was pale and almost translucent while her silver straight hair hung lifelessly, falling in a sleek but limp curtain around her face. Her eyes darted to Telara's glowing Rotary before she looked back at Telara. Telara felt a chill travel down her spine as those eyes seemed to stare right through her. "Hello, Telara," the woman spoke, her words soft but they carried on the wind so that Telara could hear them.

"What do you want with me?" Telara demanded.

"Just to talk," the woman assured her.

"Yeah, right." Telara glared at her.

"You don't believe me?" The woman smiled at her, a smile that on the surface looked benign although Telara refused to be fooled. So many times, she had been fooled. "What have I done to make you ever doubt me?"

Telara gave her an incredulous look. "You're one of the bad guys. Helloooo." Telara held out her arms with fingers splayed wide. "I can't believe that you'd seriously ask me that. You want us dead."

The woman laughed. "You have been fooled, my dear. All that you've been told is a lie."

Telara snorted. "As if I didn't already know that. If that's what you came here to tell me, then you should've saved yourself the trip."

"So, you aren't interested in hearing the truth?" The woman asked her.

Telara sighed, "and I suppose you can tell me it all, only if I join you? Am I right?" When the woman didn't respond she shook her head and used her Rotary to form a glowing rope she intended to snare the woman. The rope circled the woman but yet the woman didn't seem to look worried.

Telara jerked on the rope to make it tighten but it just dissipated, which brought a frown to her face.

The woman laughed again, "they give you weapons only designed to stop the shadowy creatures but not someone with greater power. I'm not a shadow, I'm as human as you are. All I want is to return to my home and my throne."

"Who are you?" Telara clenched her hands.

The woman watched Telara closely, her fingers laced together in front of her while her head moved to her side. "Exactly what do those fools at the Sanctuary tell you about who you truly are?"

"That we're born with powers that we use to defeat the Shadow Master and his Magine." Telara left out the part of their death, she wasn't sure why.

"That is all?" The woman queried.

Telara lifted a shoulder. "You tell me."

"I may be very knowledgeable but there are still some things that even I don't know." The woman countered. When Telara remained quiet, the woman gave a soft laugh. "You're a tough nut, you know that?" She gave a sigh when Telara still said nothing. "So, which one of you has the power of the mind?"

Telara had done her best to keep her expression neutral, but when the woman asked that question, she couldn't help the slight tightening of her jaw.

"I hit a mark?" The woman looked pleased with herself. "Would that be you?" Telara felt it odd that the woman asked that. Zane knew she had the power of the mind, Zane knew all their powers. He taught them so much in the Prime rooms back in Haven, how did this woman not know that.

"What I want to know is how you don't know that?" Telara asked her, her hands sliding into her pockets.

"What do you mean?" The woman tilted her head, her expression serene and thoughtful.

"You and Zane work together, correct?" Telara asked.

The woman nodded.

Telara smirked. "Seems team Shadow doesn't communicate well." The woman's eyes narrowed, which only made Telara's smile grow.

"I guess it doesn't matter what side you're on, communication always seems to be a problem." The woman admitted. "So, how did Lucius and the others handle hearing that you had the power of the mind?" She asked a bit too sweetly for Telara's liking.

"What do you mean by that?" Telara asked her suspiciously, not trusting the direction this discussion was going.

"They fear the power of the mind, so they must fear you. The power of the mind is the most powerful ability; you can bend reality." The woman told her while walking slowly back and forth, her eyes watching the dark smoke wall around them. "You can't tell me that you haven't sensed that, unless," she paused and cocked her head with a thoughtful expression. "You must not have inherited your mother's empath ability." The woman spoke slowly, though her words confused Telara.

"Empath? I'm not an empath." Telara frowned at her. "Look, who are you really?"

"My name matters not but it seems that your friends refer to me as the Magine. Though, I'm not sure why." The woman's face looked puzzled but she frowned when Telara jumped back.

"That can't be." Telara gave a shake of her head.

"What can't be?" The woman asked.

"The Magine is supposed to be some type of monster that regenerates between Guardian cycles." Telara stared at her. "Not some woman who works with the Shadow Master."

"Why? Because those in Sanctuary told you this?"

"Lucius told us," Telara told her.

"And he's never lied to you?" She gave a triumphant smile when Telara's lips tightened. "Thought so, that son of mine isn't very forthcoming with the truth. He likes his secrets."

"Son?" Telara's eyes widened. Things were slowly falling into place for her, all that they've learned from the trips to the past, the play at Haven, and what I.Q. had learned from the Stargazer. The Paladins came to Earth to bring back Lucius's mother who fled here, who would also be Zane's grandmother, and also the person they called Larsa during one of her trips to the past. Even as things started to come together, she realized there was still much she didn't know.

The woman nodded, "He is, although he wasn't lucky enough to be gifted with the power of mind. I believe it was that jealousy that led him to betray me, and try to vilify me." The woman gave a shrug. "Children can be rather finicky."

"Don't tell me, you'll forgive him for his betrayal if only he joins you." Telara said, her voice dripping with sarcasm.

The woman threw back her head and laughed. "Oh, that'll never happen, I promise you. I don't forgive betrayal from anyone." She told her. "I have suffered much betrayal, something I'm sure you understand. Why should we forgive those who betray us? Why should we be the bigger person? Why is it never the person who's the perpetrator that has to be the bigger person? If given the chance, I'd end his pitiful life."

Telara's eyes went wide. "But he's your son!" She protested, I.Q.'s words about Lucius writing that his mother had killed her mother and husband coming back to her.

"And he betrayed his mother, so his kinship no longer applies." The woman told her with barely a care. Her eyes moved again, to Telara's Rotary that glinted. "I only want those loyal to me on my side. Those who are against me, are nothing more than mere bugs to me."

"What do you want with me?" Telara asked her.

"Just to give you a friendly warning about the crystal witch you've been chatting with."

"What crystal witch?"

"The one who visits you in your dreams."

"How do you know about that?"

"I know about a lot and I know she's only looking out for herself as she's always done, once she gets what she wants she'll turn on you just like the others have." The woman moved closer. "Don't trust her and I wouldn't give her what she wants if I were you."

"But, you're not me and I don't trust you."

The woman grinned, "I knew you were smart, after all, you are my great-granddaughter. Listen to me or don't listen to me, the choice is yours. I only wanted to warn you." She turned away but Telara stopped her.

"That is why you're here? To just warn me?"

The woman turned to her. "That is all."

"You're the great evil, why would you want to help me?" Even as they learn more and more, there's still so many unanswered questions.

"Very good question, and here's another, why is it the ones they claim to be evil, are the only ones telling you the truth?" She smiled when Telara frowned at her. "When you find out the answer to that question, you'll have all your answers and be able to end all of this for yourself and your friends." With those words the darkness engulfed them both. When it disappeared, Telara was standing there by herself on the street in the Hills.

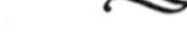

"You seem distracted."

Pam turned sharply, heart skipping as she spotted Larsa standing a few feet away, her gaze sharp and unreadable. "I'm not distracted. Just thinking," Pam replied evenly.

Usually, she stayed out on the porch, safer there, away from the Shadows that slithered and drifted through the house like smoke with eyes. They never touched her, never hissed or snarled, but their presence still coiled around her like a reminder, she had chosen this side. Or rather, pretended to.

For now. Pam thought to herself.

Tonight, she'd chosen a different corner to think in. A long-abandoned room, maybe once a dining area in a different life, now filled with broken chairs, layers of cobwebs, and a lounge chair flipped on its side. No mirrors. No distractions. Just space to breathe.

"Thinking about your so-called friends?" Larsa asked, voice calm but edged with something sharper.

Pam's brow creased. "What do you mean by that?"

Larsa studied her for a beat, the corner of her mouth twitching in something that might have been a smile. "Nothing against you. But true friends… don't they stand by your side no matter what? They don't judge. They reach out. Fight for you."

Pam kept her face still, but something twisted low in her stomach.

"Have any of them reached out?" Larsa added, almost gently.

"They don't know where I am," Pam replied quickly, too quickly. Her fingers curled slightly at her sides. "They can't."

Larsa arched a nearly translucent brow. "You're saying they couldn't find you if they really wanted to?" Her voice was delicate. Apologetic, even. "Forgive me, I meant no offense. I was only thinking of you."

Pam said nothing. Inside, her thoughts spun in a dozen directions. Was this part of the game? Was Larsa just probing for cracks in her resolve? Or… had her friends really given up?

Stop it, she warned herself. *She's trying to plant doubt. That's what she does.*

But still…

After a long pause, Larsa inclined her head with a

respectful nod. "Forgive me for interrupting your... pondering. I'll leave you to it."

And with that, she turned and glided from the room.

Pam remained where she stood, staring at the doorframe long after Larsa had gone. Shadows whispered somewhere down the hall, but she stayed still. Watching. Thinking.

That woman is dangerous, she told herself. *And worse—she's good at it.*

18

"WHY ARE the bad guys trying to help us out?" I.Q. asked looking up from the battered book he had been reading, the one Drake gave him in Alaska. "None of this makes sense." They sat along the back wall at Hallowmere, having spent their morning in the training halls and now were relaxing at a table. They no longer avoided the other Arions that were walking around Arcadia, they no longer just waited to die. Now, they wanted to find out what it was that they didn't know.

"That has become the norm for us." Tia scoffed. "So tired of not knowing who to trust and who will turn on us." They all nodded in agreement. "I'm really ready to end this."

"And keep our lives in the process would be nice," Cole inserted.

"Have you found anything in that book about the Primordial Key yet?" Vanna peered over I.Q.'s shoulders, squinting at the book.

"I'm not sure," I.Q. lifted a shoulder in a shrug. "There is that crystal tier hierarchy that I was telling Big Time about. The top one is called Primal Crystals."

"Primal Crystals? But you said the Primordial Key wasn't mentioned." Telara said.

I.Q. nodded. "It doesn't say that directly, but this book does say that only the Primal Crystals can bridge the veil between the realms." I.Q. said flipping through the book.

"Really?" Chance leaned in. "Does that mean that they used the Primordial Key to cross the realms?"

"Would explain why Larsa would want it." Vanna interjected.

They looked at I.Q. who was reading through the book. After a few moments of silence, I.Q. looked up to realize that they were still looking at him. "What?" he asked, looking confused momentarily, but at their looks he realized that question was meant for him. "How would I know? I wasn't with them when they crossed the realms."

"Even our past selves weren't with them." Telara pointed out. "The Stargazer talks about our births here on Earth." The others nodded.

"The book also talks about the colors of the crystals." I.Q. said as he continued to flip through the pages.

"What about 'em?" Vanna asked as she grabbed a chip from the bowl that one of the gnomes who worked at Hallowmere, put on the table.

"Says a crystal of pure color is more powerful than one of mixed colors." I.Q. put the book down and grabbed a chip of his own.

"Really?" Cole frowned and looked down at his red crystal. "I thought ours were colored due to our powers."

"What about the others?" Tia looked over at him with a raised brow.

He shrugged. "What about them? They don't have powers."

"And yet theirs are colored too." Vanna frowned at him.

"They are?"

Vanna slapped her forehead with her hand at Cole's question but when Tia slapped him, she realized he was grinning at her. "You're a jerk." Cole leapt out of his seat when a vine slapped him, he frowned at Vanna but she just smirked at him.

"So, does the color of the crystal mean anything?" Telara asked I.Q., ignoring them.

"Doesn't really say anything about specific colors, just the shades of the colors." I.Q. flipped a few pages before he looked back up. "The darker the crystal, the more powerful it is. The lighter, the more mute the power." I.Q. looked back at the book, his eyes moving as he seemed to read. "Although there's a passage that claims that while the power is more mute, it can also be just as powerful if not more, depending on the situation."

"Situation?" Chance's brow furrowed. "What does that mean?"

I.Q. shrugged. "It doesn't go into any other detail. Though it does say a black crystal is the most powerful, although it gives a warning that they can also be the most volatile and must be handled with care."

"Just like the crystal essence." Chad grinned, straightening up in pride.

"Actually, there is a list of uses for crystal essence." I.Q. noted. "One is imbuing a power into a muted crystal, which makes that muted crystal more powerful."

"Situation," Vanna nodded.

"Ahhhh." Chance grinned. "Now I get it."

"So, why did everyone at Sanctuary claim it was so dangerous?" Telara frowned.

"Everyone except for Claw," Cole pointed out. The others nodded in agreement.

"Because, they didn't have this book." I.Q. held up the book.

Telara sighed. "Still feels like we're just getting half the information."

"Half is better than none." Tia pointed out.

"Sometimes." Telara sighed and stood up. "I don't know about you guys, but I'm ready for some of Lin's cooking, then bed." There was a chorus of agreements as they left Hallowmere.

PAM MOVED QUIETLY DOWN THE CORRIDOR, HER BOOTS SCUFFING the cracked tile as the usual trio of tiny Shadows darted past her feet, giggling and shoving one another. In the year she had been here, she had grown used to the little ones, though in the beginning they had knocked her over more times than she cared to admit.

They were deceptively small. At first, she'd feared they were children. After all, she knew that some of the Shadows here were actually Arions. And these Shadows were childlike in size and energy. Zane and her brother had quickly disabused her of that idea.

"They're true Shadows," Zane had said with a grim look. When she pressed for more, his expression darkened, and he walked away without another word. That had been enough for her. She didn't ask again.

Still, she kept her distance. Not that it mattered. Wherever she went in this cursed place, those three always seemed to show up, either already waiting or arriving shortly after. The smallest, the one Pam thought of as the girl of the trio, was always humming that strange little tune while the other two danced or mimicked her movements. She didn't know if they were siblings, but since they were inseparable, she thought of them as such.

Pam stopped when she realized where her steps had taken her, Larsa's room. The wooden door stood quiet, its iron handle cold under her fingers. She hesitated, then raised her hand and knocked. No answer.

After a moment's pause, she pushed the door open.

She wasn't sure what she expected; a collection of ancient books, cursed relics, maybe some hint to Larsa's true motives. But what caught her attention instead was a single object on a small writing desk: a flower.

A crystal flower.

She recognized it immediately. Her breath caught. It looked like the same type of flower her brother had once given to Stazi. She knew Flint had taken it from Stazi's office during the Shadow attack on Citadel, knew it had hurt Stazi that he'd done that. Was that the same one? If so, why was it on Larsa's desk?

"Were you wanting something?"

Pam spun, her heart lurching, to find Larsa standing in the doorway, her arms hanging loosely but with eyes narrowed; not angry, exactly, but sharp and unreadable. Pam drew on her training from her years as Alpha Leader, she stared right back at Larsa while she collected her bearings before she answered. "You did invite me to visit anytime I wanted to chat." She pointed out.

Larsa nodded while she moved past Pam into the room. She took off her long cloak that she usually wore and hung it on a hook that was nailed to the wall just behind the desk. Larsa sat down on the chair and turned to face Pam who was staring at the flower. Larsa smiled and lifted the flower out of the vase. "Do you like my flower?" She asked as she twirled the flower between her fingers with a smile. "Your brother gave this to me."

Pam stiffened, her body reacting before she could stop it. She felt the twitch in her jaw, the catch in her breath, but she made no move, said nothing.

Larsa didn't notice, or at least pretended not to. "Would you like to hold it?"

Pam shook her head, politely but firmly. "It's lovely, but no thank you."

Larsa replaced the flower gently in the vase. "So," she said, folding her hands in her lap, "what shall we talk about?"

Pam pressed her lips together, her mind working quickly to come up with something to say, that hid the fact that she was actually in here to snoop and not talk. "Family." She said, as something stuck with her from the chats she had before with Larsa.

"Family?" Larsa asked her quizzically.

"You mentioned once that you understood what it felt like to fight for family; even when they don't fight for you." Pam reminded her.

Larsa gave a small, almost sad smile. "Ah, yes. I remember."

"I was just curious, who could hurt someone as powerful as you?" Pam asked. "Unless I'm overstepping my boundaries, I'll leave you in peace if that's the case." Pam put in hurriedly and even moved as if to leave the room in emphasis of her words.

"No," Larsa said gently, waving her down. "It's all right." She gestured to a chair Pam hadn't noticed behind her. "Sit. Please."

Pam sat slowly, trying not to look as wary as she felt.

"My betrayal didn't come from siblings. I was an only child," Larsa began, her voice growing quieter. "My parents died when I was very young."

"I'm sorry to hear that." Pam said.

Larsa dismissed the sympathy with a flick of her hand. "My mother barely noticed me; she spent her days staring into nothing. My father… well, he wasn't around much." Her expression remained composed, but Pam noted the glint of steel behind her words. "It was my son who betrayed me."

Pam's eyes widened.

"He blamed me for his father's death. And he punished me by taking away my only grandson."

"That must have been… difficult," Pam said slowly.

Larsa nodded, her eyes briefly distant, then she smiled again, too quickly. "Eventually, I overcame it. On her deathbed, my mother confessed that the man I'd believed was my father wasn't, in fact, my true blood. That truth led me to someone else. My real father."

Pam blinked. The more Larsa spoke, the more this sounded like something out of a twisted family drama.

"My grandson came to see things differently in time," Larsa continued. "We've been… healing. Together."

Pam's mind reeled. The implications were huge. Was she talking about Zane? Was he the grandson? It'd explain a lot of things.

Before she could press further, Larsa stood, brushing invisible dust from her skirt.

"I'd love to continue," she said with a pleasant smile, "but I'm very tired. Let's talk again soon, this has been rather therapeutic."

Pam stood too, forcing a polite smile. "Of course."

Larsa opened the door for her. "Sleep well, Pam."

Pam stepped into the hallway, her heart thudding.

Was any of that real?

It was a story carefully told, with just enough emotion and detail to make it sound plausible, but something about it didn't sit right. The flower. The grandson. The way Larsa made herself sound like a victim.

Pam didn't trust her. Not for a second. But she couldn't deny how clever the woman was. She'd woven truth and lies together so tightly that Pam wasn't sure where one ended and the other began.

And worst of all… something told her that not only was the story not over, but was going to get much darker.

19

Lucius stood silently in his stone prison, arms folded, his eyes locked on the shifting portal. Through the veil of shimmering light, he watched as Pam exited Larsa's room, her expression clouded, her steps hesitant. Something passed between them; a glance, a whisper of manipulation. He narrowed his eyes.

"What game are you playing, Mother?" he muttered under his breath. As if in answer, the portal's focus shifted, centering on Larsa's face. Her eyes flicked toward him; not at the portal, but through it. Lucius held his breath. A small, knowing smile tugged at the corner of her lips, the kind she used when she had outwitted an opponent before they even knew they were playing.

His jaw tightened. He'd seen that smile in his childhood; on the nights when she returned from so-called meetings and stared into the fire for hours, silent and unreachable.

The image warped and blinked out.

"It seems your mother doesn't want anything to do with you," came a cool voice. "Not very motherly, is she?"

Lucius didn't startle. Instead, he turned his head slowly to the side. Persephone stood beyond the barrier, her presence as ethereal as it was unsettling. She looked exactly as she had the last time; flawless skin with a grey undertone, silver laurel gleaming faintly, her eyes a dull mirror.

"Hello, Persephone," he greeted, dry as ash. "Lovely to see you again. You're correct on that assumption, she's never been very motherly."

She gave the barest tilt of her head. "Larsa does seem... selfish. Not the nurturing type."

Lucius gave a slight nod, then stilled, something in her tone catching like a splinter under skin. His gaze sharpened. "I wasn't aware you were... acquainted with her."

Persephone's hand ghosted along the stone walls, fingers trailing as though recalling a memory buried in the rock itself. Her voice was delicate, like silk stretched over blades. "You wouldn't be the first man to underestimate me." Her eyes met his, flat and glinting. "And you won't be the last."

Lucius arched a brow. "How often does Hades underestimate you?"

A sound, faint as wind brushing over a tomb, slipped past her lips; laughter, perhaps. But there was no joy in it. No amusement. It was hollow, like it had been practiced long ago and forgotten how to feel.

Lucius studied her with growing discomfort. The legends always spoke of Persephone as the jewel of spring, the reluctant bride, the lady who brought life back to the world each year. This woman was shadow-wrapped and cold, her smile a thin facade stretched across something darker.

"My husband," she said at last, "chooses to believe that I'm blind to his... indiscretions. I allow him that comfort."

Lucius's gaze turned to steel. "And yet here you are, watching me, speaking of my mother with intimate disdain. When did you first meet her, Persephone?"

She didn't answer. Instead, she tilted her head, as though considering how much to say; or how much he already knew.

He leaned back against the wall, folding his arms again.

"You knew her before Sanctuary fell, didn't you? Before the Paladins vanished. Before any of the Guardians were born."

Still, silence.

Lucius narrowed his eyes. "Was it your idea to separate the children? To bury the truth so deeply even the gods forgot it?"

A flicker. So faint most would miss it. But Lucius saw it.

A breath too slow. A twitch at the corner of her mouth. Not quite a frown. But a crack in the mask.

Then, without a word, she vanished.

Lucius exhaled slowly and looked back toward the dead portal, his mind racing.

"Right," he murmured. "I thought so."

TELARA LAY IN BED AWAKE, HER MIND SO BUSY WITH ALL THAT they have discovered and all that they have yet to discover. She stared at the ceiling, missing her little squiggly friends right now. When her mind wouldn't let her sleep back in Sanctuary, those little guys and their actions would help her fall asleep. She turned over and stared at the wall, wishing she had answers to all the questions that were keeping her awake.

What was the Primordial Key and what did it do?

Who was Kyler and what did she want?

Who was Larsa and what did she want?

What was Pam trying to do and why didn't she tell them?

And most of all, how did they die?

With a deep breath she closed her eyes, silently willing herself to let those questions go so that she can get some sleep. Some much-needed sleep so that her mind will be sharp tomorrow, she had a feeling things were about to come to a head, and she didn't want to be sleepy when that happened.

"Hello Ti…Telara."

She turned around to Zane standing there in front of her, she frowned at him, then looked around her. They were standing in Sanctuary, although not the old one with all the treehouses and the tent that housed their command center. She turned to him and frowned, crossing her arms. "How is it that you're able to hijack my dreams?"

Zane shrugged, walked away from her to look over the stone wall that bordered the crystal caves.

"Could it be the familial ties?" she asked him, watching his shoulders straighten. "After all, you wanted to call me Tien, didn't you?"

He turned with a smile, his eyes bright. "You remember?" he asked, looking excited.

She gave a shake of her head. "No, but I've been taken down a memory road that isn't mine."

His smile dropped and he sighed. "It is yours and yes, our familial ties let me visit you in your dreams. Something you get from your mother; her people are the mystics of our realm."

"My mother lives in Michigan and doesn't even remember me anymore, all because of this!" Telara shouted, her arms outstretched to encompass all around them.

Zane breathed in deeply. "That's something I blame my father for. He shouldn't have let you stay with them for so long."

"Lucius?" she asked him, her arms crossing once again.

Zane nodded.

"Hades has him," she told him.

"What?" Zane seemed shocked to hear that.

"Hades took him prisoner, we don't even know if he's alive or not." She watched him carefully, but there was no sign of anger, only a quiet, contemplative stillness.

"Why?" Zane murmured to himself. "Unless…"

"Unless?" Telara prompted him.

Zane shook his head. "Nothing you need to worry about, Tien." Before she could protest him calling her Tien, he continued, "My father has played both sides of the fence for so long, it was bound to come back to roost."

His words made her forget her irritation at him calling her Tien. She tilted her head one way, then the other before she said, "You don't seem worried."

Zane gave a humorless laugh. "If you knew my father as I did, you wouldn't either. My father is a survivor and will always survive. Even if he paints his son as the monster," he grumbled as his lips curled.

"You work with the woman who killed your friends and your wife!" Telara stared at him in amazement. "And yet you try to tell me that you don't want the death of me or my friends? Talk about playing both sides!"

"How do you know that Larsa killed my friends and your mother?" he asked her, watching her closely.

Telara lifted a shoulder. "It was either her or you; you tell me," she countered.

"It was the gods," he countered right back. "They cursed my friends and your mother. They killed you and your friends."

"Except for Zach," Telara pointed out.

"You said his name before," Zane spoke slowly. "At the time, I wasn't sure who you meant. Zach is the twin of the one you call Cole." She nodded at his remark and he continued, "They are the sons of Kull, the blowhard himself." Again, she nodded. "How do you know he wasn't killed?" he asked her.

"Well… we don't really. But we do know that he wasn't resurrected with the rest of us," she informed him.

"Hmmm…" He looked thoughtful. "I wonder what happened."

"So do we." Telara lifted her lip in a wry grin.

Zane looked at her and reached out for her, but when she

stepped back, he gave a heavy sigh. "I wish things could be different, Tien. I wish that you didn't have to go through all that you're dealing with. I wish none of you Guardians had to deal with it. I'm trying to help save you guys, I know you don't believe me," he said, holding up his hand when she opened her mouth to respond. "You don't have to believe me, but I hope you know I do love you."

Before she could respond, the world around her started to disappear and she was back in her bed. She sighed and closed her eyes. "But yet, still no concrete answers. Why am I not surprised?"

"Another dream invasion? You should start collecting rent," Cole joked the next morning. They had finished breakfast and were heading to Lumenhall. Jerry had been gone for a few days, Lin said he had some managerial stuff to take care of, but other than that was very vague about his whereabouts.

"Ain't that the truth," Telara said with a crooked grin.

"Wonder what he meant by Lucius playing both sides?" Vanna mused.

"Feels like just another riddle to me, honestly," Telara shrugged. "No one seems to want to tell us exactly what they mean or why. Kind of tired of that."

The others nodded in agreement with her.

"Sounds like Zane believes that Lucius is a bad guy," Cole mused.

"Or he's just a son that's mad at his father for not believing him," Tia shrugged.

"Or a bit of both," Telara said.

"He said the gods killed us," I.Q. started, but then corrected himself. "Our past selves. Do you believe him?"

"I don't know, not like that isn't possible. The gods have always done petty shit." Telara commented. "I wouldn't put it past them, but without any concrete evidence, we can't really say that's what happened."

"We need to figure out how we died and lay that question to rest, so to speak," I.Q. said, then chuckled as he realized what he had said.

"Do you really think that if we figure out how we died, that it'll be the answer to everything?" Vanna asked him.

I.Q. gave a half-smile. "I honestly don't know how much it'll answer, but I've a feeling that it'll be a big start. It might even be the catalyst that we need, to end the war with the Shadows."

"And saving our lives?" Chance asked.

Another half-smile. "Maybe, but we won't know until we figure it out."

"Think the answer is in that crystal book of yours?" Telara asked.

I.Q. gave a shake of his head. "I don't believe so. I think the answer to the Primordial Key is in there, but not the answer to how we died."

"So, where do you think that answer lies?" Telara asked him.

He grinned at her. "Zach."

"Zach?" Telara's brow furrowed.

I.Q. nodded. "Yup! I have a feeling if we could just get all of us together again, that we might be able to remember exactly what happened to all of us."

"So, we just have to wait until Zach decides to visit all of us in our dreams again?" Telara gave him a disbelieving look. "We don't know when that will be."

"I say that we bring him to us," I.Q. responded back.

"How?" Telara asked him as they neared Lumenhall.

"If Zane can hijack your dreams due to your familial ties, why can't we?" I.Q. countered back.

"I don't have any familial ties to Zach, though." Telara gave a shake of her head.

"I do," Cole spoke up.

I.Q. pointed to Cole in confirmation. "Exactly. You and Zach have ties because of your past relationship, but Cole and Zach are twins. What blood could be stronger than that?" He looked over at Chad and Chance. "Remember those twin tests you guys did back in grade school?"

Chance nodded. "Yeah, we're complete opposites but yet we picked all the same answers. Found out that despite our differences, we had a deeper and stronger connection."

"Bingo!" I.Q. said with a smirk.

"How do I call him?" Cole asked warily. "I've never done anything like that. What if I call him but can't call you guys?" He started to sound nervous.

"Why don't we all crash in one room tonight," Telara suggested. "Cole concentrates on Zach and I'll concentrate on the rest of us. See if that works."

"It can't hurt," Tia agreed.

"Then it's decided." I.Q. gave a sharp nod and big grin. "Tonight, we invade someone else's dream for a change."

"I like the sound of that," Telara grinned.

20

Telara was walking by herself from Lumenhall, heading towards Jerry and Lin's home where the others were waiting for her. Kasey had stopped her when they were leaving, asking her to help one of the crystal researchers with some crystal essence that they couldn't touch. Telara could use her power to handle the essence for the researchers, so that no one could get harmed.

Telara looked around her as she walked, pausing when she realized that Henry was lumbering along right next to her. She grinned and continued with the gator following her. "Thanks for the escort, Henry."

"Have you thought about what I said?"

That voice! Telara turned to see the woman standing there watching her, the woman who wouldn't tell her who she was, but she knew. "Hello Larsa," she said simply. Henry moved closer to Telara, giving Larsa a baleful look.

The woman's eyes narrowed on her. "Impressive."

Telara shrugged but said nothing. Just stared back at Larsa silently.

Larsa looked down at Henry when he let out a chuff in her

direction, she gave a dismissive look and turned back to Telara. "Have you?"

Telara frowned at her. "Have I what?" She sent out a mental warning to the other Guardians, but she couldn't feel their thoughts.

"This conversation is just between you and I; we'll keep the other Guardians out of it." Larsa informed her.

"And If I don't want it to be private? If I don't trust you?" Telara countered.

Larsa gave a small snort, her eyes moving down to the Rotary on Telara's wrist before she spoke. "I don't see where you've much of a choice, although considering that you put your trust in friends who betray you consistently, don't you think that you could give me the same consideration?"

Telara glared. "You're no friend, you want me dead."

"You keep saying that, but yet I don't remember ever saying such a thing. You listen to those that continue to lie to you and keep believing their lies." Larsa said to her, while her gaze continued to keep moving between Telara's face and her Rotary.

"So, the deaths of the past Guardians are lies?" Telara asked.

"They died at the hands of the Shadow Master, as you can see, I'm no master." Larsa held out her hands.

Telara could keep going back and forth with this, but she knew it wouldn't be helpful. "Why are you here?" she asked instead.

"I want to talk," Larsa said simply.

"Then talk." Telara stayed where she was, feeling better with Henry in front of her.

"I know how it feels to be betrayed. I've been betrayed by my own family, it hurts and it makes you do stupid things. I've done some stupid things in the past but now, I'm ready to make amends."

Telara's eyes narrowed on her, waiting for Larsa to look

up from her Rotary to her face before she responded, "Really? Why do I feel my Rotary comes into play with your plans?" Telara hadn't been for sure, but the way Larsa kept looking at her Rotary, she felt safe challenging Larsa on it. From the widening of Larsa's eyes, Telara felt she had hit a bullseye.

"Don't you want to go back to your normal life? With your real parents?" Larsa asked and continued, "The parents who raised you, not the ones who walked away from you?"

Telara had to admit that it sounded tempting, she missed her family, but she also knew that Larsa wasn't trustworthy. "You can do that?"

Larsa nodded with a triumphant grin. "Give me the Rotary, as you call it, and I can make that happen. There'll be no need for a final fight, we can end this now."

"What about my friends?" she asked.

"They'll return to their families, like none of this ever touched them," Larsa promised, her lips stretching into a smile that might have passed for kind, if it didn't make Telara think of a snake in a storybook, coaxing a child toward its coils.

"Even the ones from Sanctuary?"

"Even the ones from Sanctuary." Larsa nodded, still smiling.

"It's a lovely fantasy," Telara said, her voice quiet and slow. "But there's one problem with it." She watched as Larsa's triumphant demeanor began to crack.

"And what's that?" Larsa spoke with a barely controlled irritation.

"It doesn't come off," Telara said simply, her posture tensing as she watched Larsa's eyes widen. "I don't even know how I got it on."

Larsa frowned at her. "What do you mean it doesn't come off? Of course, it comes off!"

Telara lifted her arm and attempted to pull it off with her

other hand, but the Rotary didn't budge. "No, it doesn't. So, even if I wanted to, I couldn't give it to you."

Larsa's mask of feigned friendliness crumbled, her expression twisting into something far darker; anger, or perhaps pure hatred. "Then we'll see if it will stay on your dead corpse," she hissed, lunging at Telara in a blur of motion. But before she could reach her, Henry lashed out—his tail snapping through the air with surprising speed and force, slamming Larsa backward.

The impact bought Telara just enough time to rise into the air, levitating off the ground as she commanded her rotary to conjure a shimmering shield around herself. "I'm not going to be that easy." Telara glared right back at Larsa.

"But you're all alone, and I'm not." Larsa taunted her as it grew darker around them, Shadows moving from their hiding places to stand next to their mistress.

"She's not alone."

Tia's voice was a welcome sound, when she turned, she saw Tia standing there with the other Guardians, all had their Crims drawn and their suits already forming. She turned back with a grin, and with a simple touch, she was suited up.

Larsa moved back as the Shadows converged towards the Guardians. "Get me that Rotary!" Larsa said with quiet malice.

Telara moved forward, her Rotary shield growing in size. "I'd like to see you try." She braced herself for the Shadows that started towards her, their only target the Rotary on her wrist. Each Shadow moved with ease, changing shapes from animals to even trees.

"These ones aren't created from Arions!" Telara grinned.

"Static!" Cole moved forward, twirling his nun chucks, the handles glowing faintly with ember-like warmth. His body lit up with flames as he leapt through the air, flame balls shooting from the nun chucks hitting a handful of Shadows that exploded into black smoke. Shrieks could be heard from the dissipating smoke.

Tia threw her hands wide, a sudden gust blasting the smoke clear from Cole's blast. She twirled her whip around her, creating a whirlwind that lifted her off the ground. She moved forward as other Shadows lurched towards Telara. "You're not getting near her!" she shouted. With a flick of her wrist, her whip sliced through a diving Shadow with razor-sharp precision. Another one that dissipated into black smoke.

Vanna crouched low, pressing her staff to the ground. "Let's see how they handle Mother Nature." Roots burst from beneath the soil, wrapping around the remaining Shadows, yanking them back and keeping them from their objective. "You're not going anywhere."

Chance lifted both palms as he pulled the water from the pond that swept over the road and doused the Shadows that had almost reached Telara. The Shadows stopped and stumbled.

Chance chuckled. "They must not like getting wet."

His brother followed behind him and slammed his sword into the ground, freezing all the water on contact. Spikes of ice erupted upward, freezing the Shadows in mid-leap. "They definitely don't like the cold."

I.Q. jerked his arm down, his Crim turning into the electrified bow in his hand. He lifted it up and pulled back on the string, a lightning arrow forming. "Let's see how they like the shock." He let the arrow go and with a loud crack, the arrow exploded the Shadows it connected with.

When the air cleared, only one Shadow remained. Telara moved forward, her Rotary changing from a shield to a whip in her hand. "You're not getting my Rotary!" She spoke with cold determination as she moved forward. Her and Tia leapt into the air, each one taking a limb with their whips and holding on even while the Shadow screeched out in pain.

Vanna brought up vines and roots to hold it still as it struggled while Chance drenched the Shadow and Chad froze it in place. I.Q. shot his electrified arrows while Cole flung fire balls at the Shadow that exploded into black smoke. The blast sent them flying to the ground but when they looked up, the smoke was already dissipating. Telara looked around but Larsa was also gone. She slammed her hand on the ground. "Dammit!"

"Hey, next time." She looked up to see Tia holding her hand out, with a grin she took it and let Tia help her get off the ground.

"Thanks!"

"Seriously?" They turned to see Trevor, Jeff, and Stazi standing there with their Crims in hand. "You're telling me that we missed all the fun?" Jeff looked at them with a frown.

They all erupted into laughter and fell back against the cold, wet ground. "Next time, we'll wait for ya." Telara said between breaths.

"Truly?" They looked up to see Gage standing there, watching them.

Telara bit her lip and nodded at him. "Truly!" she said and grinned. "This isn't just our fight, and I'm sorry that I forgot that for a bit."

Gage gave a shake of his head. "Don't sweat it, just remember that you said that," he told her.

"I will," she promised.

He nodded. "See you guys tomorrow." They nodded as they watched him walk away with Trevor, Jeff, and Stazi.

She turned to the others smiling. "Come on, we have a dream to invade."

They laughed and linked their hands as they walked to Jerry and Lin's home, together. Along the way, Telara told them what Larsa had said.

"Did she tell you why she wanted your Rotary?" I.Q. frowned, looking at Telara's Rotary.

Telara shook her head. "Nope, just made promises about giving us our lives back but when she found out that I couldn't take it off, she tried to kill me for it."

"Do you think she could've done what she was promising?" Vanna asked.

"I don't think so." Telara shook her head.

"What makes you think that?" Cole cocked his head and looked at her.

"Because, if she had that power, why wouldn't she just use it to make it so that we never became the Guardians? If we hadn't become the Guardians, I would've never received the Rotary, then she could've taken it herself." Telara said, kicking a stone in the road.

"Except that everyone seemed surprised when the Rotary attached itself to you," I.Q. mused. "You said it yourself, you didn't truly pick the Rotary, it more like called to you."

She nodded. "That's true." She looked down at the Rotary. "Maybe this isn't a normal Crim after all, but if it isn't, then what is it?" She looked up at them.

"I don't know," I.Q. told her. "Maybe that mystery is wrapped up in the mystery of our deaths."

"You think so?" she asked.

"I don't think I've ever said I don't know as much as I have since we first came to Sanctuary," I.Q. grumbled and the others laughed.

Chance grasped I.Q.'s shoulder. "Don't worry, bud, you're still the smartest one out of this bunch." The others nodded and laughed. "Let's go see if we can find some answers in our dreams."

21

With Vanna's room being the largest one, they grabbed blankets and pillows from their rooms and that's where they camped out. Her bed was big enough for all three girls while the boys camped on the floor and Cole took the chaise lounge chair that was in her room.

"So, all I do is just think about my brother as I fall asleep?" Cole asked as he settled against the back of the chaise lounge.

They all looked at I.Q. who was settling into his makeshift sleeping bag. When he felt their eyes upon him, he looked up and frowned. "Why is everyone looking at me? I've never done this before; this is all just a guessing game right now."

"So, what's your best guess?" Vanna asked him.

"That Cole concentrates on his brother while Telara concentrates on us, and if it goes the right way, we'll all open our eyes in a dream with all of us there." I.Q. said as he lay against his pillow. "It might not hurt if the rest of us try to concentrate as well. Hopefully, see everyone shortly," he said and closed his eyes.

Cole closed his eyes and they could hear him chanting under his breath, "Zach...Zach...Zach..."

Telara breathed in deeply and closed her eyes, concentrating on each of them, doing a silent mantra in her head, repeating all of their names. Thinking about each of them, and how she wanted them to join her in her dream. She wasn't sure how long she lay there concentrating, but with a groan she sat up with frustration. "I don't think this is working," she grumbled then froze.

"Welcome back," Zach grinned at her.

She looked around. "Where are the others?"

"Here!" Tia and Vanna walked out of the nearest tree house while the boys walked out from a tent.

"All here!" Cole grinned and clasped Zach's shoulder. "Hey bro!" Then he looked at the others with a big grin. "I did it!"

Zach looked at him and smirked. "Sure, you did."

Cole's smile faltered as he turned back to Zach. "What do you mean?"

Zach gave a small shake of his head. "Nothing." He grinned and walked over to Telara. "Hello, Tien," he spoke.

"No, no, no," Cole said, walking after Zach. "You can't just say something like that, then walk away, what did you mean by, sure, I did."

Zach laughed and turned to look at Cole. "You're still so easily goaded, brother." Everyone laughed and nodded. "You take after our father in that."

Cole's expression darkened when Zach said that. "I take nothing after that jerk."

Zach's expression went from amused to bewildered. "Jerk?"

"We've met Kull," Telara said in a measured tone, not wanting to make this situation worse. "Him and Cole didn't really hit it off. He was a bit of a jerk," she admitted with a regretful look at having to admit that to Zach.

Zach gave a look of understanding. "I've heard that he could be, but I've never met the man, not that I remember. He disappeared when we were babies." He sighed and looked at

Cole. "Sorry, your experience with our father wasn't a good one."

Cole shrugged. "Hey, his loss." Then his expression lightened. "I ended up with a brother so, I'm good."

Zach nodded in agreement, then turned to Telara. "How are you doing?"

She smiled at him. "I'm doing good, but we really need to find out how we died."

Zach frowned. "I don't know," he admitted with a lift of his shoulders. "What makes how we all died, so important?"

"We think it might help us stay alive," I.Q. supplied.

"How?" Zach asked them.

"If our calculations are correct, the reason that our past selves get sent to their deaths, is to hide the details on how we were killed." I.Q. grimaced. "I know, kind of morbid. It's just a hypothesis right now, but it's all we have to go on."

"I wish I could help," Zach told them. "But, I've no idea what happened to us."

Tia sighed and looked over at Telara. "So, what now?" she asked her.

Telara opened her mouth to speak, but before any sound escaped, Vanna gasped.

They all turned sharply, eyes widening at what they saw. There, standing before them, was the singer from the concert they took Pam to; the enigmatic lead singer of The Cray.

Varnak.

"Whoa," Cole breathed, shaking his head as if trying to dispel a vision. "What's going on?"

Telara glanced at Zach, but his face mirrored their confusion.

Then Varnak spoke, his voice exactly as they remembered it; smooth, melodic, otherworldly. Soft music curled through the air around him, as if the very atmosphere played for him alone. He wasn't singing, yet his every word carried the rhythm and gravity of a song born from time itself.

"It's time.
The sleepers must awaken.
Their slumber is done,
And the past calls."
They glanced around, frowning as the very air around
them began to shimmer; thickening, wrapping them in
something unseen, like a velvet fog pressing in from every
side.
"The wheel turns,
The curse stirs,
And what was buried must now be unearthed."
Telara tried to reach for Zach's hand, but her fingers felt
numb. She couldn't move. None of them could.
"Ashes of old truths stir,
The weight of lost names calls,
And blood sings the song of before.
Their eyelids grew heavy, and his voice, like wind through
ancient trees, slipped into their ears and settled deep within
their minds.
"Let the Guardians recall their names of old,
Let their hearts break for what was lost,
And let the fire of remembrance burn away the veil."
His words didn't just echo; they *possessed*, threading
through thought and memory until they became all that was.
"Only in truth can they rise,
Only in pain can they be reborn,
Only together can they stand against what comes."
The world tilted, slowly spinning out of sync with reality.
Yet they remained standing, caught in Varnak's spell.
"Walk again the path once taken.
Face again the wounds once borne.
And find again the selves you were meant to be."
The final syllable lingered like the last note of a song,
fading into silence.
And then... darkness.

One by one, they fell, as if tugged by invisible threads, vanishing into the past that waited to be remembered.

Telara opened her eyes, rolled over, and pushed up from the ground to stand up. Looking around she saw the homes that were built into the trees, doors of all sizes built into the trunks. She saw them during her trips to the past but they were just doors to her then. Now, she remembered it all. She knew it all. The smallest tree with the pink door is where Cleo lived, a small female gnome who liked to weave flower wreaths.

"I know this place." Telara turned to see Chance walking and looking around with wonder. "We played Petteia over there." He pointed to a tree stump, with two smaller ones next to it, where they saw the board game with the small pebbles they used.

"Yeah, you cheated that last game we had." Chad looked at Chance.

"Tien." Telara turned and smiled at Tia before they hugged one another.

"Chantria." Telara smiled, grateful that even in the past they were still close.

"Brother." They turned to see Zach and Cole embrace one another. Unlike Chad and Chance, they weren't identical, but you could see the resemblance now.

"What are we supposed to do?" Vanna asked, walking around while flowers sprouted from beneath her feet.

"Jacinta, you're worried," Zach told her and motioned towards the flowers.

Vanna snorted. "Of course I'm worried. I remember everything but how I died."

"Tien! Zach! Zeke! Guardians!"

They turned to see Nikos running to them. They had very few mortal friends, after Kull sent the twins to Sanctuary with a warning about the Gods turning on them, they had kept all of them in Sanctuary. Very few mortals were allowed past the barriers. Nikos was one of the few. He had been orphaned at a young age, so their parents had taken him in, and he became a dear friend.

"Nikos!" they all greeted him.

"Want to play a game of Petteia?" Chad asked, then frowned at Chance. "I need to play someone who doesn't cheat."

Nikos shook his head, attempting to catch his breath. He turned to Telara. "I heard some of Ares warriors talking, they spoke of your grandfather."

"My grandfather?" Telara asked him. "Lucius!"

Nikos nodded, still breathing heavily. "Yes, when they noticed me, I had to run. They threatened to cut off my head and put it on a stake."

"My grandfather, what did they say about my grandfather?" Telara asked, her heart clenching.

"He's being held down in Tartarus by Hades. We need to tell the Paladins; they need to go save him." Nikos insisted.

"Our parents aren't here," Zach said slowly, looking at Telara who was shaking her head.

She looked at Zach with tear filled eyes. "We can't leave him there, Tartarus is full of torment, I can't leave my grandfather to Hades."

"We won't!" I.Q. said, his body sparking with his power. His electric bow forming in his hand, no Crim needed.

"How are we going to get there?" Zach asked. Before anyone could respond the ground beneath them rumbled as it rose up and cocooned them. They turned to Vanna who smiled back at them.

"We're going there in style," she informed them as they felt a drop in the air as she pulled them beneath the ground. The grassy ball opens up and they see the Asphodel Fields in front of them. They saw souls of the undead walking around with unseeing eyes. Vanna shivered.

"Why did you drop us in Asphodel Fields, why not Elysian Fields?" Chad asked her, rubbing his arms.

"Do you really think that Hades is hiding Lucius in Elysian Fields?" she countered and Chad grimaced in agreement. "At least I brought us up past Cerebus." A distant growl had them all feeling thankful for that.

"Let's go find my grandfather." Telara moved forward but Zach grabbed her arm.

"Let's be cautious about this," he spoke and knelt down, placing his hand on the ground. Without asking, Telara knew that he was listening to the ground, that he could hear for thousands of miles by a mere touch. Zach could manipulate sound waves to work for him, and right now, he was listening for Lucius. He looked up at her with a frown. "He's not here."

"What do you mean?" Telara frowned at him.

"'Tien!" She turned when Tia called her name, her body going tense. They were surrounded by the little demons that roamed Tartarus and all of the underworld. Different sizes, some with horns, some whose horns looked as if they had been torn off, and most with claws and fangs.

"Silly, silly, kids." One of the demons spoke with its scratchy and screechy voice. Tilted its head and looked at them with its beady black soulless eyes. "Come running without thought and now you're at our mercy." There were many demons there watching them, walking through the lost souls as if they weren't there. The demons all stared at them, their claws clicking together while their tongues would dart out and lick their sharp teeth.

"Down, heathens," the voice sounded regal, though cold. They turned to see Persephone move through the demons, who parted to create a path for the Queen of the Underworld.

"Persephone, you kidnapped my grandfather?" Telara asked her, knowing she asked that same question long ago. They were walking in the exact footsteps of their past selves.

"I know nothing of your grandfather," Persephone told

her, in that same cold voice, still moving with deliberate slowness towards them. "You're trespassing in my realm."

More rustling had them looking around to see others moving in the shadows. Minor gods and goddesses they knew from their teachings. Melinoe, the daughter of Persephone and Zeus or Hades, no one truly knows. The fact that she's the goddess of ghosts and madness, made many believe that her father was Zeus. One side was completely pale white, while the other was black as night. She stayed close to her mother, though her eyes never left them.

Dolos, the spirit of trickery and deception, floated over the demons, moving closer to them with his mad smile. His eyes glazed with madness, fingers that resembled claws and a cloak that hid most of his transparent form. They knew to keep their distance from him, with Melinoe it took only a touch to drive someone mad, but Dolos could do it with just a thought.

Hecate, the Goddess of witchcraft, moved amongst the demons, her torches in hand while her dark gaze watched them. Hypnos stayed off to the side, his wings flat against his back.

"We may have provoked a force far greater than we're prepared to withstand," I.Q. muttered, his grip tightening on the crackling bow of lightning in his hand.

Each Guardian moved forward, since their memories had returned, their powers had become second nature. They had no Crims, but they needed none, not here. Cole created fire in his hands, Chance lifted himself on a small wave of water, vines and withered tree roots swayed beneath Vanna and a wooden staff was presented to her by the roots. Chad created an icy sword in his hand and Tia had her wind whipping all around her. Telara felt a vibration and turned to see Zach's body vibrating with his sonar abilities.

"We need not fight today." Persephone spoke as she

continued to move through the demons, her eyes on Telara. "Not as long as you give me what I want."

Telara frowned. "And what's that?" Not trusting Persephone, she kept her body tense and ready to fight if needed.

"We want the Crystal Heart," Persephone told her. "The final part to the Primordial Key."

Telara had been about to tell her that she didn't know what she was talking about, but then she looked down on her wrist. There was the Rotary, a crystal of great power that had chosen her when she was young. She had called it such, due to the fact that the crystal rotated within the confines of the liquid metal that encased it. "And what happens if I were to give you this... Crystal Heart?" she asked, her hands clenching into fists.

"We will complete the collection, create the Primordial Key, and Hades' little tart can go back to her home and leave Hades to me." Persephone spoke in her cold, calculated tone.

"What happens to us, when that happens?" Telara asked her, eyes darting around them.

"I don't know and I don't care, give me the crystal now!" Persephone's voice rose slightly, though still carried its frigid cold tone. Hypnos moved closer, watching them with great interest. "What I do know is that if you don't give it to me, you will die now."

"Sorry," Telara told her. "Actually, not really. You're not getting it." With those words Telara lifted herself from the ground, her Rotary glowing and expanding to cover them all.

"We'll see about that!" Persephone raised her hand. "Kill them all and bring me that crystal!"

The demons rush towards them as well as the gods and goddesses. Hecate turned Vanna's vines against her, muttering words and incantations that they couldn't understand. When Cole attempted to rush to her rescue, he was ambushed by several demons that leapt upon him, biting and clawing at him.

The smell of burnt hair filled the air as Cole managed to set two of them ablaze. When another leapt at him, Telara created a barrier that the demon bounced off of. Cole nodded and ran towards Vanna who was at that moment being pulled underground. The area glowed brightly, with each word Hecate spoke.

"We need to take out the witch goddess," Telara shouted before she was knocked out of the air by a vision of a shadowy attacker. She crouched on the ground trying to find the attacker only to be attacked from behind. She looked up into the faceless attacker and realized this must be the work of Dolos. A wave of sound filled the air and a force rolled over them all, sending their attackers away.

"You keep taking our fun away, not very gentlemanly of you," Hypnos appeared behind Zach, grabbing him and pulling him away from them, into a dark portal that appeared. "Let's take you out of the equation."

"No!" Telara ran to him but it was too late, he was no longer there. When she turned around, she saw that Hecate was still chanting, and that the other Guardians were encased within her glow, as their powers turned against them.

Persephone was getting closer to her, a cruel smile forming on her lips. "You're all on your own, now. I'll have what I want, then you can join your friends. Hades wishes be damned."

Before Persephone reached her, a figure appeared between the two. A gorgeous male with blond hair, perfect figure, and radiant smile. He stood before Telara, facing Persephone.

"Adonis, what is this?" Persephone demanded.

"I can't let you do this; I love you but this is wrong and you know it," he told her.

"I don't care," she responded.

He gave a sad sigh. "But I do." He turned to Telara. "Go back to your parents."

She attempted to protest, to demand he free her friends, but was blinded by a bright light. When it dissipated, she was standing in Sanctuary, her parents turned to see her with relief shining in their eyes.

"Tien, oh how we worried." Her mother smiled and held her arms open.

Before Telara could move, she felt a presence behind her; cold, ancient, and heavy as stone. Her parents' eyes widened in horror. She turned around.

Hecate stood there, her gaze a void of endless black. No hatred. No mercy. Just the stillness of death.

A sharp pain ignited in Telara's chest. She looked down, trembling, and saw the burning shaft of one of Hecate's torches impaled through her. The flames licked at the fabric of her chiton, searing flesh and cloth alike, while her blood spilled in rivulets, pooling at her feet.

The world seemed to tilt.

She felt Hecate's hand reach for the crystal on her wrist, but it vanished in a shimmer of light. The goddess recoiled with a shriek of fury.

Telara coughed, blood flecking her lips, but managed a weak smile. "You failed. You'll never get the Key now."

Hecate's expression didn't change, her eyes looking around them both before turning her gaze back on Telara. "All we need is time," she said coldly.

Pain tore through Telara's body, white-hot, then fading fast. The warmth fled from her limbs. A freezing numbness crept in.

And then Hecate's voice echoed, as if from deep underwater, hollow and final. "Bound by blood, sealed by fate; until the Key is born, you shall die to live, and live to die."

A scream, raw and primal, cut through the haze around Telara.

Her mother.

Telara's head turned with effort. She saw Marsella crumple to her knees, her wail shaking the air itself. Grief pulsed from her like a storm, and with it came something darker. A wave of shadow burst outward, swallowing the stone beneath their feet.

Plax stepped into view; confusion etched across his face.

Too late.

The darkness surged over him, engulfing him, and from that black tide rose the first true Shadow. Around them, more forms clawed their way from the earth. Silhouettes of despair and rage, drawn by Marsella's broken heart. The Shadows moved toward her crumpled figure, toward the source of their birth.

Zane held Marsella in his arms, his face carved in grief, silent and unmoving.

Telara wanted to scream, to warn them, but her voice was gone. Her limbs were lead. Her vision dimmed. Then she saw them, Kala and Kali, rushing in, desperate to help.

She wanted to cry out to them, to tell them to stop and run away. But the words wouldn't come. And then, Melinoe appeared behind the twins.

All it took was one touch. In an instant, Kala and Kali vanished, stolen away before Telara's fading eyes.

Her heart gave one last stuttering beat.

Then all was dark.

TELARA JERKED UP, HER HANDS GOING TO HER CHEST, BUT THERE was no wound there. Looking around she saw the other Guardians waking in the same panic. Their eyes darted around, their breathing heavy, and their bodies shaking.

"I couldn't breathe," Vanna gasped looking around.

"I could feel the burn of my own fire," Cole said, tears shining in his eyes. "I have never experienced something so painful."

I.Q. gave short, jerky nods. "It was as if our powers were turned on ourselves."

"Hecate," each of them spoke that name like a curse.

"We know how we die," Tia said, tears falling down her cheeks as she held her knees to her chest.

Telara looked down at her Rotary and grimaced. "And now, we know why. They wanted my Rotary to complete the Primordial Key."

"Which means they have everything else they need, we just don't know what it is," I.Q. spoke, still breathing hard. "But, at least, we know the one thing they don't have."

"How is it that they didn't get it when you were killed?" Chance looked at Telara and for a second, she frowned but then remembered, they weren't with her when she died.

"It disappeared from my wrist before I died, then Hecate chanted some words," Telara said slowly, her tongue darting to wet her lips. "And that's not all." She told them all about what happened, how her mother created the Shadows, how Plax was caught in that wave, and how Melinoe appeared behind the twins and they disappeared.

"So, that's how they became Crazy Mary," Chance shook his head. "Well, we have the answers we were looking for and some others, but what now?"

"Now?" Telara sighed. "Now, I'm getting up, not going back to sleep anytime soon. We can worry about what's next later. Right now, I want a shower."

They all nodded in agreement and left for their own rooms.

22

THE HOUSE of the Shadows was quiet when Pam returned from her walk, none of the normal activity she was used to seeing. After her discussion with Zane, she needed to take a walk to clear her head, the house felt as if it was suffocating her. He sounded so earnest, as if he truly believed everything he's doing is for the benefit of her friends. She wanted to believe him; she wanted to believe that her presence here wasn't for naught. He promised her that her actions were to help her friends and that soon she'd be reunited with them. She just couldn't shake the lingering feeling as if she was missing something, something that was important.

She moved swiftly up the rickety steps and through the front door, still no movement from inside. She had no destination in mind when she entered, so how she ended up in front of Zane's door, she had no idea. But there she stood, right in front of his door. She lifted her hand to knock on the door but instead, with a twist of her wrist she was inside the room. She was done asking permission, she was done worrying about her friends, she wanted to know what was going on, and she wasn't going to stop until she had the answers. She wanted to be with her friends; she was tired of all these cloak and dagger games that Zane seemed fond of. She needed to be there for them, not only to help them but because she needed to be there because she missed her friends.

She paused in the open doorway, her brow furrowing as she looked around the empty room. Well, unless you count the Shadow that looked at her from behind the bars of its cage. She moved into the room, looking around but still no sign of anyone. The oversized chair in front of the fire sat empty, as was the wooden chair behind the desk. She turned to see the Shadow staring at her intently from his cage. "Where is he?" She asked the Shadow who tilted its head at her words. "Yeah, didn't think you'd answer me." She muttered but then to her amazement, the Shadow lifted its dark arm and pointed with one of its black claws to the doorway. She snorted and gave a humorless laugh, "Not happening, bud. You want free, you talk to the Shadow Master himself." When the Shadow continued to stare at her, she decided it was time to leave.

Moving out of the room into the hallway, she paused and breathed in as she looked down the empty hallway. Where was everyone? What was going on? She asked herself silently. Looking down the hallway, she tilted her head as she realized that was the way to Larsa's room. It was also the same direction that the Shadow had pointed. Was that Shadow trying to tell her something? She peered back into Zane's room but the Shadow had already turned its attention elsewhere. The Shadows never seemed to be able to concentrate on one thing for too long. With a deep breath she moved from Zane's door and down the hallway towards Larsa's room.

She reached out to the handle, her hand grasping it lightly before she pulled back. She didn't feel any fear or dread about entering Zane's room but for some reason, her body tensed about entering Larsa's room without permission. She straightened her back and knocked sharply on the door, straining to hear if there was any noise from within. After a few moments, no one spoke up, so she turned the knob and entered Larsa's room. No one there, all she could see was the desk, chair and the crystal flower that Flint had given to Stazi so long ago. The crystal rose that Flint stole back from Stazi, then given to Larsa, her lips thinned as she continued to stare at the rose.

A roaring sound filled her ears; she couldn't pull her gaze from the rose and wasn't sure why. A roaring that made it impossible for her to concentrate on anything except for the rose. All she could see was the rose, her vision seemed to darken around the edges. A roaring that rose in volume, the darkness around the edges of her vision growing with the noise. She thought of all that she had been taught about the Guardians from a young age, how it jaded her opinion of them so that when they came to Sanctuary, she wanted nothing to do with them. But they weren't like the Guardians that her parents spoke of, they were different. They became her friends, friends she wanted to help. All that they had done to try to stop the prophecy of their death coming to fruition, nothing seemed to make a difference. Zane and her brother telling her how, as long as she went by Sanctuary's rules, she'd never be able to truly help her friends. The hurt she saw on Telara's face when she went back to Sanctuary for Zane. Those thoughts filled her mind until all the hurt, anger and resentment came boiling to the surface.

She grabbed the crystal rose and with all her might she sent it flying across the room, against the wall on the other side. With the shattering of the rose as it fell to the dirty floor, her mind cleared and she felt as if she could breathe again. Her body sagged against the table as she felt deflated now that her high emotions had deserted her. She looked over at the broken crystal pieces on the floor and couldn't remember what had compelled her to throw it the way that she did. As she stared at shattered pieces she frowned, a purple haze started to form, growing in size until it became a solid form kneeling over. She watched the form rise up and turn towards her. She pulled out her Crim that shifted into a staff, as she watched the woman warily, unsure of what was going on.

The woman rose and smiled at her, her blue eyes bright and her blond hair long. She wore a purple robe that resembled the outfits worn by ancient Greek women. "Hello." The woman said kindly.

Pam looked around the room, making sure they were the only ones there, then turned back to the woman warily. "Hi."

"Thank you for freeing me; I'm sorry about manipulating your emotions to create such anger." She breathed in deeply, then released slowly. "I have no excuse for doing such a thing to you except that I wanted my freedom, but that doesn't give me the right to bring you such angst."

Pam opened her mouth to respond but closed it while breathing out. "Ummmm." Her brow furrowed as she attempted to put her thoughts into words, the only problem was that her thoughts were so jumbled, there were no words for them.

"I'm sure you have many questions," the woman said, to which Pam nodded. "I wish I could answer them all for you but I fear we're needed in a place called Arcadia."

"What do you mean?" Pam wasn't sure what the woman was talking about. "Who are you?"

"I'm sorry," the woman said with a regretful expression. "I'm handling this all wrong, being imprisoned in that flower for as long as I have, has made my communication skills rather unsteady."

"How long have you been in that flower?" Pam asked.

"Too long, my name is Marsella, and Larsa is the one who imprisoned me within the crystal flower. I don't know how the flower came to be in the possession of your brother, it seems there are periods in my memory that are lost to me. But during my entrapment, I've been somewhat conscious and able to see as well as hear most of what has happened around me."

"Oh. I'm so sorry you've had to go through that, sorry that my brother had anything to do with it." Pam spoke, although she wasn't sure why she was apologizing, but knowing she truly felt bad for what Marsella had gone through.

Marsella shook her head. "You have nothing to be sorry for, and neither does your brother. I told you that so that you would understand why I'm saying we need to go help your friends." Marsella sighed. "Larsa has lost patience with the Guardians. She used her soul crystal to summon all the Shadows to Arcadia. My family and your friends are in grave danger."

"We need to go then." Pam moved out of the room and down the hallway.

"Hold on," Marsella told her outside of Zane's office. "I have one thing I have to do before we leave." Pam frowned but followed Marsella into Zane's office where the Shadow in the cage seemed to get excited upon seeing them return.

"Ummm, what are you doing?" Pam asked her when Marsella moved towards the cage.

"I'm righting an old wrong." She said as she reached for the latch on the cage door.

"Not even Zane can control that Shadow," Pam protested as Marselle opened the door and the Shadow moved forward, staring right at her.

"Of course, Zane couldn't control him," Marsella knelt down, her voice breaking as she stared at the Shadow. "I'm so sorry, Plax. I never meant for any of this to happen." She moved forward and hugged the Shadow to her, Pam tensed in her fighting stance as she watched the Shadow, worried for Marsella. Something that she needn't have been. As she watched the Shadow started to glow brightly, just as they had

when Vanna had healed them. Although this seemed different, in the glow she could see the form of a male forming until
he stood over Marsella. As Pam watched, the male lifted
Marsella from her kneeling position on the floor and
embraced her.

"But Vanna couldn't heal him," Pam shook her head. "How
could you?"

Marsella wiped at her eyes before she turned to Pam and
gave a sad smile. "Vanna couldn't heal Plax because the
power that turned him into a Shadow wasn't a false power.
The same reason that Zane, or even Larsa, could control him.
I could heal him, because it was my power that changed him."

"You turned him into a Shadow?" Pam frowned when
Marsella nodded. "But, why?"

"There are many questions that I'm sure you have, and
they deserve answers, but right now, we need to get to
Arcadia and help your friends. When it is done, I'll answer
any questions that any of you have. It's time to end Larsa's
reign." Marsella told her.

"I'm for that," Plax agreed. "It's time for that witch to go
down for all that she's done."

"How are we going to get there?" Pam looked around.

"We go how Larsa and her Shadows travel," Plax told her
and moved out of the room. They traveled down the stairs
and passed the rooms where the other Arions stayed. He
moved through the room where Pam knew the Arions would
gather to relax and visit with one another. An area that she
hadn't truly checked out, as she didn't want to feel as if she
had truly become a traitor. When Plax came to a back wall
with no opening or a door, Pam frowned and looked around.

"Why are we here? There's nothing here but tables and
chairs?" When she looked back to Plax she gasped. The wall
he had stood in front of, was no longer there. She was now
looking into a room with a porter, an exact replica of the one
back in Sanctuary. She stared at Plax who was already

moving to the platform. She joined both him and Marsella but frowned, "we don't have anyone to start up the porter."

"Close your eyes," Plax told her. She watched him flick an ice projectile from his fingers towards the console before she hurriedly covered her eyes.

23

LUCIUS SAT on the stone bench in his cell, leaning against the frigid wall as he watched the shimmering portal before him. Through it, he could see the Guardians walking through Arcadia, unaware of how close danger truly was. He trusted Jerry to protect them... but still, he longed to be there. To finally tell his granddaughter the truth; no more secrets, no more hiding.

A chill slithered through the chamber, more biting than the usual cold of Tartarus.

Lucius didn't need to look to know who had arrived. Still, he turned and saw her standing just beyond the threshold.

Persephone.

Her pale gown rippled like mist around her ankles; her heavy woolen cloak draped elegantly across her shoulders. There was a sharpness in her poise, a quiet cruelty behind her stillness.

"Well. Still brooding, Lucius?" she said, her voice lilting with false amusement. "So noble. So tragically... trapped."

Lucius's gaze darkened. "Come to gloat, Persephone? Funny, history always paints you as the sweet young maiden stolen away by the king of darkness. I don't see it."

Persephone's back straightened, chin lifting as she stared him down. "You know nothing of what I've endured."

"I know the Guardians never harmed you," he growled. "And they sure as hell don't deserve to be sacrificed just to protect your husband's dirty little secret."

She laughed then, a brittle, hollow sound that echoed around the stones like breaking glass.

"Worried about your little Guardians?" she asked. He didn't answer, but the tension in his jaw and eyes was all the confirmation she needed. "You should be. Your mother has plans for them. Especially your granddaughter."

Lucius sprang to his feet and stepped as close to the edge of the warding boundary as he dared.

"You think you're in control of her?" he snapped. "Larsa doesn't work with anyone. She uses people, manipulates them, and discards them when they're no longer useful. You're just another piece on her board."

Persephone's lips curled faintly, though her gaze remained unreadable. "Oh, Lucius. You poor, oblivious soul. Do you really think I don't know who she is? Unlike you and your bleeding-heart family, I know how to deal with creatures like Larsa. If anyone's being played, it's her. I'm the one pulling the strings. I arranged the disappearances of your Paladins to draw out your precious Guardians."

"Why? They were trying to take Larsa back to our realm where she'd face justice for her actions," he told her.

Persephone gave a small feminine snort. "Hades wouldn't have let you; I needed her to leave on her own. She refused to leave without that crystal key; she had one part and needed the others."

Lucius narrowed his eyes, a storm brewing behind them.

"Your granddaughter had one, though she refused to part with it." Persephone lifted a shoulder. "She went to her death believing that she thwarted us, but we had the last laugh. Hecate set them on the path of being reborn, until the crystal showed itself again. As for sending the Guardians after Larsa; either they kill her or she gets that crystal. Either way, I will be rid of her."

Lucius felt his blood go cold at what he had just learned. What he had played a part in, without knowing who started it all.

"As for the other." Persephone stepped closer, her voice low and cold. "I was able to get what your mother couldn't, from the only one your mother truly feared, Kyler, the so-called Crystal Witch. The final crystal. The last piece of the puzzle. I have it. And when Larsa collects the other two, I'll give her this one. And then she'll leave. She'll be out of my realm and out of Hades's heart."

"You're sending her back to my realm with the very weapon she's been hunting?" Lucius's voice sharpened with disbelief. "She'll tear it apart to build her kingdom on the bones of the innocent." He shook his head slowly; sorrow etched across his features. "You'd let millions suffer just to win back your husband?"

Persephone met his eyes, her voice like ice cracking across a frozen lake. "I don't care how many fall. As long as she's gone, the cost is irrelevant."

Lucius stared at her, sickened.

"Persephone... what have you done?" A deep rumble echoed through the chamber as Hades materialized beside his wife. His face was unreadable, but his eyes moved sharply from Lucius to Persephone.

Persephone turned to face him, her posture rigid, eyes still glinting with defiance. "I handled your little problem, since you wouldn't."

Hades stared at her, disbelief flickering in his expression. "How could you?"

She stepped closer, voice rising with emotion. "How could I? How could you? You tore me from my home, made me your queen, then couldn't even stay faithful? Don't lecture me, husband. I regret nothing. Can you say the same?"

Hades shook his head slowly. "Larsa was blamed for those deaths—"

Persephone's laughter cut through his words, interrupting him, sounding cold and jagged. "That child is no innocent. She cared nothing for you, just as she cared nothing for her own mother, the siren without a soul." Hades flinched, but Persephone pressed on. "All Larsa ever wanted was power. She leapt at the chance to eliminate her enemies and rule unchallenged. You think she loved you? She used you."

His face tightened, fury rising like a storm. "You know nothing of her. Or her mother."

Persephone scoffed. "I know enough. And I know what she really wanted…" She raised her hand. Nestled in her palm lay a crystal wand, six inches long, glowing with an ethereal rainbow light.

Hades inhaled sharply. "Where did you get that?"

"From the Crystal Witch who foolishly thought you loved her. While she fretted over your darling Larsa, she never saw me coming." Persephone closed her fingers around the wand, holding it close to her chest. "I made a deal with Larsa. And it's about to be fulfilled."

Hades' voice thundered, his form growing with his rage. "Give that to me!"

Flames licked the air, dark smoke billowed out from his skin. Persephone stood her ground, her glare seething. "Don't you dare to command me."

Hades erupted, his form towering, fire roaring around him like a living tempest. For a heartbeat, Lucius saw something rare in Persephone's eyes; fear. It was gone in a blink. With one last venomous look, she hurled the crystal at Hades. "This isn't over, husband," she spat before vanishing into the shadows.

Hades caught the crystal mid-air. As the flames receded,

his body shrank back to normal size. Though he held the prize, he looked weary; wounded not in flesh, but in pride. He turned toward Lucius. "You're free to go." His voice was flat and clipped, sounding barely above a whisper.

Lucius stepped forward cautiously. "Hades…"

Hades raised a hand to silence him. "Don't. Leave before I change my mind."

Lucius hesitated. "What about the crystal?"

But Hades vanished in a plume of smoke, leaving only silence behind.

TELARA GRINNED AS SHE WATCHED VANNA SPRINTING ALONGSIDE Henry, the massive gator who had once made them all uneasy. Now, he was practically a beloved team mascot, though one with very large teeth. Vanna laughed, ducking under a low-hanging branch while Henry galloped awkwardly but happily beside her, his heavy tail thudding the earth like a playful drumbeat.

"Careful with the other alligators," Jerry had warned them that morning. "Henry's tame, some of the rest aren't." They promised him that they'd be careful, but it hadn't stopped the group from enjoying their rare downtime in Arcadia. After reliving their deaths, they just needed to play around, not have to think about what they're expected to do, or what was coming their way.

Vanna zigzagged too close to the edge of the pond, lost in the moment, and her foot slipped. She let out a squeak, her arms pinwheeling. But before she could tumble into the murky water, a massive lily pad-like leaf shot up from below, forming just in time to catch her. It hovered in the air briefly, graceful and firm, before lowering her gently to the ground.

"Show-off," Telara called, laughing as Vanna gave the leaf an exaggerated curtsy.

I.Q. grinned and twirled a spark of electricity between his fingers, then sent a harmless jolt at Cole's back, making the fire-wielder jump and spin around. "You're gonna pay for that," Cole said with a smirk before launching a burst of flame just above I.Q.'s head. Tia, not to be outdone, conjured a sudden gust of wind that sent leaves swirling around them like a mini tornado.

Even Chad and Chance got in on the fun, ice and water forming a slick track on the grassy field as they tried to trip each other up, laughing like kids at recess.

It felt good. For a moment, it felt normal.

Then everything shifted.

Henry stopped dead in his tracks. The playful energy evaporated in an instant as he lifted his snout and sniffed the air. A low, rumbling growl vibrated from his chest, deep, guttural, and wrong. Without hesitation, the gator turned toward the pond that wound through Arcadia and slipped into the water, his bulk vanishing with barely a ripple.

Telara's smile dropped.

Her friends had already gone still, all of them instinctively moving closer together. No one spoke, but they didn't need to. The air had changed, heavy, electric, as if the world itself was holding its breath.

"You guys feel that?" Vanna asked quietly, eyes scanning the tree line.

"Shadows?" Chance asked, reaching instinctively up for his earring.

Chad shook his head slowly, his eyes narrowed. "No. This is different." He turned a slow circle, hand tightening into a fist as a sheen of frost formed on the grass around his feet. "Feels like when we fought that thing in Alaska. The giant."

Everyone went quiet.

The memory, raw, cold, and terrifying, hung between them like fog. That battle hadn't been a fight. It had been survival.

Another ripple broke the surface of the pond.

Henry didn't reemerge.

Telara looked around, her body tensing as she remembered that battle. She felt a sense of foreboding, especially since Larsa has visited her several times here in Arcadia.

Her Rotary started to glow, as if it could sense that it'd be needed soon. Each of the Guardians pulled their Crims from their relaxed mode and had them at the ready.

I.Q. held his bow tightly, the electric arrows sparking as he looked around them, posture tense and waiting. Vanna twirled her staff in her hand as she walked slowly with her gaze moving around them, the blades of grass moving beneath her feet and the trees around them seemed to echo Vanna's moves. Cole held tightly to his nunchucks as he did wrist rolls and behind the back passes while his watchful gaze stayed vigilant. Chad moved his wrist nonchalantly in circles with his sword, but his eyes belied those carefree movements as they stared around them. His brother Chance stood stiff with his flail in his hand, his gaze as hard as the others, while all of them watched their surroundings.

"If they're foolish enough to come into Arcadia, we'll be ready for them." Wind whipped around her as Tia moved to stand next to Telara. Tia held her whip's handle tightly in her hand but the thong whipped all around Tia. It whipped with the agitated wind but yet even as close as Tia was to Telara, it never once even came close to her.

"Yes, we will," Telara agreed with her as the Rotary started to vibrate. She frowned down at it then looked back up at Tia who was giving it nervous glances as well. "It hasn't done this since..."

"Alaska," Tia finished for her and Telara sighed with a nod.

"A scary sign."

The others moved closer to them.

"Whatever happens, we'll handle this together," Cole said

firmly, standing beside Tia. His flaming nunchucks blazed in his grip, unaffected by the wind swirling protectively around her. Their powers had become second nature now; partly thanks to Zane's teachings, but mostly because they remembered. Everything.

They remembered who they were.

Their families

And how they died.

Now they stood on the grass in Arcadia, tense and ready. Each held their Crim at the ready, braced for whatever was coming, though they didn't yet know what that would be.

Tia gasped as the sun dimmed, the light shifting unnaturally. Around them, shadows stretched and deepened. Looking up, they saw thick black clouds rolling across the sky, blanketing the heavens. It was midday, but the light was more like twilight.

"I don't have a good feeling about this," Vanna's lips pressed together, they could all feel her tension, it mirrored theirs.

A voice rang out, feminine and echoing in all directions. "This is your last chance!"

The Guardians spun, eyes scanning for the source.

It didn't take long.

A woman stood atop a mobile home nearby, her silhouette sharp against the dark sky. Shadows clustered around her; some perched on the roof beside her, many more lined the lawn beneath like soldiers waiting for command. Even as they watched, more emerged, creeping into view from every direction.

Some were the original Shadows, hulking, shapeless figures they remembered from their first battle at Sanctuary.

Others were the shifting, writhing, monstrous beings from the battle in Alaska.

"What the—?" Cole broke off, pointing.

To the side, three small Shadows danced in a circle, hopping and prancing as if enjoying some private game.

"Did anyone else know Shadows could have… kids?" Chance asked, frowning.

"I didn't even know Shadows could play," I.Q. muttered.

"Make your choice, Guardians!" the woman called again, her voice like a dagger across the wind. "This is your final warning. Join me… or die!"

"Enter the Magine," Telara sighed. She curled her hand into a fist as her Rotary shifted, morphing into an oblong shield that covered her forearm. It still pulsed with energy, but she felt steadier now, more in control.

So, is this the final battle? I.Q. spoke via their private mental link, notching a crackling electric arrow to his bow.

We're not ready. Vanna replied, her staff spinning in one hand as vines danced beneath her feet.

I don't think she cares. Tia said grimly.

The Crims glowed with the energy of their wielders, but so did the Guardians themselves. Fire licked across Cole's shoulders, radiating heat that didn't bother any of them. Strands of electricity arced up I.Q.'s arms and through his hair. Chance had thin ribbons of water swirling around his skin, while Chad's boots left frost in the grass. Vanna's aura stirred the earth itself, while the grass moved as if drawn to her presence. Tia floated just above the ground, carried by the winds, and Telara herself hadn't felt earth beneath her feet in moments, her mind humming with power.

They were ready.

Or as ready as they'd ever be.

Then the dancing Shadows stopped.

One by one, the three tiny creatures turned to face the Guardians, their wide eyes too knowing. It was unsettling. Too… sentient.

"Looks like the children are done playing around." Chad said aloud, forgetting the link in his shock.

"I'm more worried about the big Shadows and the crone leading them," Chance replied, his voice low as he spun his flail, water dripping from the metal, like falling tears.

A frigid silence followed.

"Did you just call me a crone?" the woman asked sharply, her voice cold as winter steel.

Way to go, bro, Chad muttered via the link. *Next time, maybe think it instead of saying it.*

The Shadows hissed and shifted, as if reacting to her mood. The woman's glare hardened, her presence swelling with fury.

"Well, what is your answer?" she demanded, voice rising. "Will you join me… or die?"

24

"You aren't killing anyone!"

Jerking around, they were stunned to see Gage standing there and he wasn't alone. They stared as the leaders of the Sanctuary factions with their teams joined Gage, even Carmen stood there dressed to the nines in her Sanctuary uniform. The Alaskan Sanctuary factions walked up as well, Paul and Wes winked at them. Big Time walked up with Claw, who was twirling his axe with a hard stare. Jayne stood between Paul and Wes, who towered over her, her glowing rope held loosely in her hands.

They looked at each other in amazement, they couldn't believe how many were joining them. Claw twirled his crystal ax once again before swinging it back to rest on his shoulder.

"There's more!" Cole pointed to where the Hunters were joining them as well as Billy and Billie with their team from Haven. He looked over at the others. "We might just win!" Stazi, Jeff, and Lucy nodded to them as they pulled out their Crims in preparation.

"I wouldn't count on it."

They turned to see Larsa standing there, a smirk curling her lips like a knife's edge. The Shadows around her pulsed and shifted, twisting into newer, more monstrous forms, each one darker than the last. All but the three miniature Shadows, who stood stock-still, staring at Telara with eerie, intelligent eyes.

"Look!" Vanna pointed and gasped.

When they turned towards where she pointed, they saw the Harlick brothers ambling from the trees that surrounded the marshes. Not only them but the sisters and even Nan from Alaska with her bulky coat of animals.

Telara's chest tightened, awe and dread clashing in her heart.

So many were answering the call, so many were risking everything.

"I know we promised to let them help," she said quietly, her voice trembling. "But I don't want them getting hurt. I care too much—"

"That isn't your choice to make," Gage said gently but firmly, stepping up to her.

"And you're our friends," added Patches as if that said it all, her Crim already blazing to life beside Jess.

"Friends stand by one another." Travis and Trevor crossed their arms, eyes resolute.

"No matter what." James joined them, his face unreadable but his gaze unwavering.

"Besides, I like the idea of having something to hold over your heads," Billy chimed in, smirking until his sister shoulder-bumped him hard. "I mean, I want something I can use as future ammunition." He amended, with a twinkle in his eye as his sister groaned.

"How is that any different than what you said the first time?" Tia asked, raising a brow.

"It isn't," he replied cheerfully.

Billie groaned and turned to Telara. "Basically, we're here, and you're gonna have to suck it up." She gave an exaggerated shrug.

"This isn't just your fight anymore," Stazi said, stepping forward. "This fight belongs to all of us."

"They're right," Vanna added, her eyes misty but determined.

Telara looked at the growing crowd of warriors, each one a thread in the tapestry of their shared story. People from different homes, realms, and histories… united by something greater than blood.

She took a deep breath and nodded, eyes glistening. "Thank you, everyone."

A beat of silence passed, a sacred moment of solidarity.

Then, Claw hefted his axe onto his shoulder, his voice a grumble that somehow held more weight than a war drum.

"Enough of this mushy, mushy crap. Let's take down some Shadows."

"Don't say I didn't give you a chance," Larsa sneered, raising her arm.

In her hand, she held a circular crystal weapon with metal inlays, unlike anything the Guardians had seen. No metal shielded her skin from its raw energy like their Crims did. The crystal looped around her palm, anchored by a glowing bar gripped in her fist. As she raised it higher, Telara's Rotary began to vibrate, humming with a strange, agitated energy.

Telara gave her arm a sharp shake, trying to steady it. The Rotary pulsed once more, then settled, but unease prickled down her spine. Whatever Larsa was wielding, it was interfering with her own Crim… and while they no longer needed their Crims to use their power, the Crims still gave them some stability.

Then, with a single downward sweep of her arm, Larsa gave the signal.

The Shadows surged forward.

The larger ones reached out with clawed limbs, trying to seize any Arion they could touch. Blinding flashes of light lit up the battlefield as Crims collided with Shadows. Screams tore through the air, raw, inhuman, and full of rage.

The battle had begun.

The air pulsed with energy as light and shadow clashed across the Arcadian fields. The cries of Shadows echoed between bursts of elemental fury; flames, lightning, wind, water. The Guardians and Arions fought as one, their powers humming through the ground like a symphony of war.

Suddenly, a familiar voice shouted above the chaos.

"We're here to help!"

Kasey came charging down the hill with Jacob at her side. Allison and Carter followed, each lugging packs of tech and gear they'd been modifying. Lillie came last, face determined, her tiny fists clenched.

Telara turned, eyes widening. "The Vanguards?"

They stopped just short of the battle line, breathing hard, eyes wide at the Shadows roiling just beyond the clearing.

"We trained with you!" Kasey shouted. "We can fight too!"

"You're not ready!" Cole called over the din, his hands aflame as he shielded a group of Arions from a swooping shadow-bird. "This isn't a game, it's war!"

"We know!" Jacob snapped back. "But we're not kids anymore!"

"Look!" Carter held up a small crystal detonator. "These can destabilize the smaller Shadows; we made them from left-over fragments and crystal essence!"

"And I brought some light grenades," Allison added. "They will clear an area fast!"

"They're brilliant," I.Q. muttered to Telara, ducking a blow from a clawed Shadow. "But—"

"No," Telara said, and stepped forward. Her voice softened. "You've already proven how brave and smart you are. That's not the question. The problem is, if we fall, we need someone else to keep Arcadia alive. We need someone to protect the ones who can't fight."

The Vanguards faltered, glancing at each other.

"Lumenhall," Telara continued, gripping Kasey's shoulder. "Get the residents out. Now. Get them into Lumenhall's deep chambers. Seal the lower levels if needed. If anything happens to us..." She looked back at the battle. "You keep them safe."

Kasey swallowed hard, her voice cracking. "You're putting this on us?"

"I trust you," Telara said, looking back at her. "All of us do."

"You want to help?" Claw added from behind, dragging a Shadow with his ax. "Save lives."

A moment passed, then Kasey nodded.

"You heard her!" she barked at her team. "Vanguards, move!"

As they turned to run, Lillie hesitated and looked back. "You'll come back, right?"

Telara gave a faint smile, one that held every ounce of hope she had left. "If we don't... make sure Arcadia survives."

Then the Vanguards were gone, disappearing through the trees, their packs clinking with tools and crystals, their mission clear. And for a moment, as another wave of Shadows crested over the battlefield, the Guardians stood a little taller.

The shapeshifting shadows moved more swiftly than the lumbering ogre shadows that moved at their own pace, their clawed hands reaching out for any of them that dared get close. The sound of a small car that ran through their legs, echoed around them as Fritz rode his mini car over the battlefield. Shadows bent to catch him, and when they would, one of the Harlick brothers would smash their head with one of their many clay pots.

Chad distracted, cheered them on, his brother using a watery rope to pull him back when a moose shaped Shadow charged at him. Chad leapt up from the ground, turning to face the moose whose head was lowered and swinging in aggression.

"Pay attention brother," Chance shouted, watching the moose warily.

"Yeah, yeah, let's just take this horse with horns down." Chad grumbled, his icy sword held in his hand.

The moose started to charge at Chad, ignoring Chance. Chance thrust both palms forward, pulling water from a pond to create a wave that crashed into the moose. Chad flipped into the air, landing on the back of the moose and using both hands, he brought the sword down into the neck of the moose. Ice crept from the wound, encasing the moose as it moved.

"Time to take this bad attitude of a moose out." Cole moved forward, skimming over the ground, the heat from his body lifting him. Chad jumped down and rolled away just in time as Cole hit the icy sculpture with a fireball and it exploded. The guys high-fived one another, then quickly turned to go join Travis and James who were battling two ogre looking Shadows.

"Have to be careful with these ones," Cole muttered. "They could be friends."

"You clean behind their ears and I'll cool them off," Chad told his brother and together they moved in unison. Chance pulled water from the ground to flower over the Shadows while Chad froze the water, effectively encasing them in ice. "Let's hope this holds them long enough."

Chance grimaced. "With this Florida heat, I doubt it." Even with the overcast the Shadows brought, the air was still warm.

"Let's worry about that when it happens." Chad rushed over to help some other Arions that were battling Shadows.

Tia, suspended on a funnel of air, danced between aerial Shadows shaped like massive black hawks. They dove at her with clawed talons, wings whispering with shadowy rage. She spun mid-air, slicing through one with a blade of wind. Another dove too close to her, she turned holding up her hands to defend herself.

I.Q. pulled back on his invisible string and shot a charged arrow of lightning at the bird, the bolt frying it midair. "Got your back!" He shouted with a wave.

"I know!" Tia grinned, spinning again, the wind forming a cyclone beneath her as she blew another hawk to the ground.

Vanna was sending her vines after Shadows that were shaped like little spiders, thankfully, Telara was nowhere around, or she'd be freaking out. Each vine would wrap around the spiders and squeeze them until they popped.

"Watch out!" Stazi yelled.

Vanna turned and vaulted over a shadowy alligator that raced after her. Touching the ground, she brought roots forth that encased the gator and held it still. "Get it!" She shouted.

Stazi leapt onto the gator, her twin blades glowing as she brought them down onto the gator who let out a gurgling shriek before it melted into black mist.

While the others battled giants and shapeshifting animals, Telara's gaze locked onto the three tiny Shadows that were watching her from a nearby rooftop. The tiny female jumped down and skipped towards her, humming a haunting tune.

Telara powered herself up, lifting her from the ground as she watched the little Shadow. From the corner of her eye, she saw the slender one, with its clawed hands slink forward on all fours, letting its claws drag along, scraping the stones. The larger one lumbered behind, snorting and grunting as it moved.

"I don't trust them," Telara turned to see Nan standing there watching the mini-Shadows with interest.

"Me neither," Telara responded to her. "Got any ideas?"

Nan tilted her head, then hurled snarling, furred beasts at the Shadows, their claws slashing and teeth snapping. The slender one moved out of the way by flipping over and continuing its movement forward. The animals hit the bigger Shadow of the three, knocking it onto its back, where it flailed and bellowed.

The female turned its head to look at the downed Shadow, still flailing and bellowing out on the ground. When it turned to look at them, Telara had a sense of foreboding, as if she could sense that the little one was ticked off and about to retaliate in the name of her little friend.

Telara lifted up her arm, creating a large shield with her Rotary in preparation but what she didn't expect was for the Shadow to let out a shriek that split the air. Telara clutched her head, the sound feeling as if it was trying to bore into her mind. She gritted her teeth and concentrated, sending out a wave of mental force. The scream stopped.

"I'm not playing today," she growled. But, the three Shadows were no longer there and neither was Nan. She slammed her hand on the ground, looking around at the others who were battling Shadows of different shapes, sizes and ferocity.

A Shadow bear rose behind Paul, who was slicing through a Shadow snake with his crystal scythe. The snake had taken Wes down, his bow flying. Paul grinned and attempted to say something but the bear slammed his back with his mighty paw, sending Paul tumbling to the ground.

She was about to run to help when Lucy leapt up on the back of the bear, bringing her batons down on its ears. She leapt back off as the bear let out a painful roar, his paws going to its head. Jayne wrapped her glowing rope around its feet and, jerking back, slammed the bear onto the ground. Trevor ran in and brought his pole blade down onto the bear; they watched as it dissipated into smoke.

They worked like a unit, no hesitation, no fear.

Across the field, Billy and Billie fought back-to-back, Crims flashing in rhythm. Claw and Big Time tore through Shadows like a storm, Claw's axe glowing as it cleaved through a moose-shaped one, while Big Time punched a hulking Shadow so hard with his hand blades that it cratered the ground when it exploded.

They were winning, Telara grinned.

25

Telara turned to see Larsa standing there, a cruel smile on her lips. Telara motioned towards the battlefield. "Seems we're doing a good job taking out your Shadows."

"Perhaps." Larsa didn't sound upset at all, her eyes never left Telara though.

"Why don't you leave and take your Shadows with you." Telara told her. "You won't be taking our lives today."

"I should thank you," Larsa told her with a sly smile, momentarily stunning Telara. "You've set me free."

"What are you talking about?" Telara deflected a tentacle of one of the shapeshifting Shadows that lunged at her. Larsa had distracted her so that she didn't see the Shadow creeping closer. She created a barrier around herself when the tentacles reached around her. She felt the tentacles squeezing her invisible barrier she had created.

"For so long, I've had to be careful that my grandson didn't see my darker tendencies because I needed him." Larsa kept speaking to her as Larsa walked around the Shadow that was attempting to squeeze the barrier harder. "But, now that I have you, I no longer need Zane." The smile that appeared on

Larsa's face gave Telara chills. It reminded her of that one serial killer from the latest thriller in the cinemas.

"There's one problem with your theory," Telara told her as she strengthened the barrier against the tentacles that kept pressing hard against it.

"And what is that?" Larsa asked her with a bored expression.

"You don't have me." Telara told her as she pressed the power within her before releasing it against her own barrier, light exploding all around her as the Shadow screamed and dissipated. She turned to stare at Larsa.

"Not yet," Larsa said with a smirk.

"Not ever!" Telara countered, her Rotary glowing and reforming her shield.

Larsa lifted the crystal that circled her hand, her fingers gripping the crystal bar that ran through the crystal in the center. "We'll see," Larsa promised darkly.

Telara looked at Larsa's hand that gripped the crystal rod, asking the question that she wondered since first seeing Larsa with that crystal. "How are you able to touch the crystal?" Telara asked, her face contorted in confusion.

Larsa let out that cold, serpentine laugh of hers. "Only mortals need to worry about touching the crystal. They're weak, while I'm not."

Telara looked from her Rotary to the Chakra crystal in Larsa's hand. "Your piece to the Primordial key?" Telara grinned at the look of surprise on Larsa's face. Good, about time they were able to surprise someone else.

Though, Larsa quickly recovered. "Persephone always did have a big mouth," Larsa told her with a smirk, then lifted her head to look around. "Regardless, I'll get what I came for, then I'll become unstoppable."

Telara jumped into the air and with a sweep of her arm she sent spears of light after Larsa who stood there until one of the spears sliced through her cape and pierced the skin of her arm. She frowned down at her arm then back up at Telara with a frown. "How dare you?" She spat at her.

Telara gave a smirk of her own and shrugged her shoulders. "I don't have an ordinary Crim either."

Larsa stared at the Rotary, her eyes narrowing on it while Telara brought up another shield to deflect a Shadow that had taken the shape of a bird and swooped down towards her. Rather than seem upset, her face cleared and looked pleased. "Maybe it isn't." She agreed, then gestured around them. "But the Crims your friends are using look pretty ordinary to me. They also look to me as if they're losing." The pleased look on her face bothered Telara. Telara frowned at her before she looked around and saw that her friends were indeed having issues.

It looked as if the Shadows had multiplied in numbers, she could barely see her friends through the darkness. Cole was being pulled down by several Shadows who were wrapping around him and suffocating his flames. Chad and Chance were both tossed several yards, hitting a tree and slumping to the ground.

I.Q. was being pulled into the pond by a shadowy tentacle, Stazi attempted to slice through with her swords but she ended up flying into a nearby park bench. A giant owl swooped and grabbed Tia with its claws while the hawks attacked. Billy was notching his bow to help her but a big boa grabbed him, pulling him across the lawn swiftly.

Vanna was standing back-to-back with Billie and Jayne, while they were surrounded by Shadows pressing forward.

"You should just give it up and join me," Larsa told her as she watched Patches and Lucy both battling one of the giant Shadows that kept changing its shape so that neither could touch it with their Crims. "Join me and I'll spare their lives."

Telara turned back and frowned at her, "If I join you, you'll destroy the world." She protested.

Larsa laughed and shook her head, "I care nothing for this

world, I want to go back to mine, there you and I can rule together."

Telara shook her head, "Are you nuts?"

"You're of my blood," Larsa smiled at her. "Together we can rule, all will bow down to us. No one will be able to stop us, but only if you join me." Larsa cajoled while Telara just shook her head slowly as she backed away from her.

"No, I won't." Telara denied her. "You're crazy."

"Look around you," Larsa gestured around them. "Your friends are being defeated as we stand here. Either way, fight me or join me, you will be defeated. But, with my way at least, everyone will live. Your choice, blood of my blood."

Telara looked around and Larsa was correct; they were being defeated. Her chest tightened as she watched Gage fighting several Shadows that kept shifting their forms on him. He was joined by Claw who brought his axe down on the giant paw of a great Shadow bear who let out a blood curling howl. That victory was short lived as a Shadow eagle swooped down to lift Claw into the air many feet before dropping him down on a group of Arions battling some of the old type Shadows. These Shadows did their best to steer clear of Vanna, who was no longer surrounded but who was now fighting shapeshifting ones who kept moving from snake to crocodile, then to bear. While all this was going on, there were those three smaller Shadows who were running and skipping around the battlefield, as if there wasn't a great battle waging.

Telara turned back to Larsa and straightened her back, "I don't care!" She shouted to her. "We'll fight you to the end, even if it's our end." She shouted and Larsa glared at her. "But, we'll do it together because that's what friends and family do, they fight for one another no matter how dire the situation is."

A familiar voice boomed across the battlefield.

"That's my girl!"

Telara spun toward the sound and gasped. Zane stood tall

among the chaos, flanked by Flint and the Arions, those they once believed had turned their backs. But here they were, weapons drawn and eyes ablaze with purpose. Zane gave her a proud grin, and for a moment, Telara couldn't find the words.

Now that her memories had returned, she saw him not just as Zane, but as her father. She remembered the warmth in his voice, the love he had for her mother, and for her. Her heart swelled at the sight of him.

"Traitor!" Larsa screeched at Zane, her face darkening in her fury.

Zane turned to her, unbothered. "I never betrayed you, Larsa," he said calmly. "Because I was never on your side." He held up a gleaming silver sphere. "Time to end this."

Things seemed to even out as she watched Zane's Arions join their friends. She watched as they fought next to each other. Flint fought beside Claw and Gage, striking down creatures that shifted forms; wolves, snakes, birds.

Telara's hope sparked again. She scanned the field and turned to Zane, concern flashing in her eyes. "Where's Pam?"

A screech from Larsa drowned out whatever he was going to say. They turned to see her running towards him with her circular crystal weapon glowing. She leapt from the ground while Zane turned around calmly, holding his hand out with that silver ball still in his palm. Before she could land her attack though, a fireball blasted her and knocked her out of the air onto the ground several feet away.

"Always pulling your ass out of the fire," a gravelly voice growled.

They turned to see Kull, Mica, Kala, and Kali stepping onto the battlefield; powered up and ready. Telara stared, overwhelmed.

Zane snorted. "If I remember right, it was the other way around."

"Yeah, well, when this is done, I'll enjoy tossing your ass in a jail cell where you belong." Kull grunted back.

"Really, guys?"

Plants began erupting from the earth, separating Shadows from Arions and wrapping around enemies to pin them in place. Mica stood between them; arms crossed with an annoyed look.

"Can we save the posturing until after we help our children?"

"Sorry, Mica," both men muttered in unison, sheepish.

Kull unleashed a blast of fire, scorching the shrieking Shadows until they evaporated into puffs of black smoke. He reached down to help Cole, but Cole waved him off and shoved himself up with a glare. The wound between them would have to wait.

Mica joined Vanna, and together they summoned nature's wrath; earth, vine, and root striking down the advancing dark. Kali fought alongside I.Q., lightning crackling through their veins as they electrocuted Shadows that couldn't escape.

Kala moved to Chad and Chance, water and ice dancing through the air like synchronized blades. The Shadows stood no chance.

Zane turned to Telara. "You ready, Tien?"

She smiled, fire and light in her eyes. "Yes, father. I am."

She launched herself skyward, sending radiant shards flying from her Rotary. Zane joined her, and with a flick of his wrist, the silver sphere multiplied; tiny projectiles launching into the swarm of Shadows, exploding in blinding bursts.

"Vanna's not going to be happy with you," Telara laughed. She recognized that silver ball; it was the same one that had once taken the shape of a mischievous silver squirrel.

Zane grinned, then turned to Tia. "Chantria, you with us?"

Tia nodded and rose into the air, wind swirling beneath her feet.

The Arions and Guardians surged as one, pushing the Shadows back, light cutting through darkness. Wisps of black smoke drifted up like a storm clearing at last.

We're doing it, Cole said excitedly through their mind-link. *We're going to defeat her.*

They were so focused, so united, that none of them noticed Larsa rising atop a monstrous Shadow. The crystal in her hand pulsed with chaotic energy, and with a guttural roar, it released a blast of darkness that birthed even more Shadows.

The battle was far from over.

26

"THIS IS ALL YOUR FAULT!" Kull bellowed across the battlefield, hurling a jet of fire that incinerated a Shadow trying to flank him.

Zane parried a blow with a silver staff that formed from his silver ball, the weapon crackling with energy as he spun around. "How in the Underworld do you come to *that* conclusion?" he shot back, irritation flaring in his voice.

"You've been working with her for how long now?" Kull growled, stomping forward, his eyes blazing with fury. "Playing both sides as usual?"

"I wasn't *working* with her," Zane snapped. "I was trying to *fix* the mess you lot made while playing hero with a temper problem!"

"Oh, that's rich coming from you," Kull sneered. "The golden boy who always thinks he knows best."

Before Zane could retort, a quiet voice broke through the chaos; serene, yet firm. "Can't you two ever get along?"

Both men froze mid-step, blinking as if they'd been struck. They turned simultaneously toward the voice. The battlefield seemed to slow as a figure walked through the smoke and drifting shadows; golden hair, piercing eyes, calm as a still lake.

"Selly?" Zane breathed, his face stunned. "Where have you—?"

"Later," Marsella interrupted gently, walking beside Pam and a tall, blue-skinned figure with pearl white hair and dark eyes; Plax, reborn and radiant with quiet strength. "We have more pressing concerns."

Zane swallowed whatever words had gathered in his throat. Kull, for once, said nothing.

Across the field, Larsa stood atop a rise, her arm raised with the glowing crystal circular weapon. Shadows writhed and surged around her like smoke made solid, and with every arc of her arm, more twisted creatures clawed out of the ground; bears, serpents, birds with wings made of razors.

"She's using my power," Marsella said softly, stepping forward. "The shadows she commands; they were never hers to wield."

Plax reached over and placed a hand on Marsella's shoulder. "It's time."

Marsella nodded, raising her hand toward the sky. A hush spread across the battlefield. Even the Guardians stopped mid-strike, turning toward her as an unnatural stillness gripped the field.

Her fingers curled, and with a flick of her wrist, the air shimmered. Larsa paused, eyes narrowing, her grip tightening on the crystal circle.

And then it began.

Darkness, the very essence of shadow, poured from Larsa's crystal-like weapon, smoke through a crack. It twisted and curled through the air, drawn inexorably toward Marsella's outstretched palm. The shadows flickered, faltered, and let out animalistic howls as they disintegrated mid-charge, leaving only trails of black mist that drifted harmlessly into the air. The other Shadows, ones that resembled the very first ones, fell to the ground, unmoving.

"No... no!" Larsa screamed, trying to resist, clutching the circle to her chest. But the crystal now pulsed erratically, dimming with every heartbeat.

"You should've never taken what wasn't yours," Marsella said quietly, her eyes glowing. "You twisted pain into power, but I was born from both."

The last of the black energy surged into Marsella's hand. A single beat passed.

And then... a loud pop echoed all around them.

With a burst of light and a sharp ripple through the magic around them, Larsa vanished, then there was silence.

The battlefield stilled as if the world itself was taking a breath.

Zane let out a low whistle, his expression a mixture of awe and shock. "Selly... remind me never to get on your bad side."

Kull grunted beside him, grudging admiration flickering in his eyes. "You're still an arrogant idiot."

Zane cracked a grin. "Takes one to know one."

Mica rolled her eyes. "Seriously? We just defeated Larsa, finally, and that's what you two go with?"

Marsella lowered her hand, her voice quiet but resolute. "It's not over. But she won't create another Shadow. Not ever again." She moved away from them all, walking with a purpose to the battlefield where Arions were helping one another, either off the ground or to cart off an injured comrade.

"Is the battle over?"

Telara turned to Chad, who stood beside her, a bemused expression on his face. She didn't blame him. The battlefield, just moments ago a roaring sea of chaos, was now eerily quiet. Smoke and shadow still drifted in the air like the memory of violence, but peace was beginning to settle.

They all felt it. That strange, confused relief. The shock of survival.

Across the field, the woman who had appeared with Pam, called Marsella by both Zane and Kull, was moving slowly between the fallen Shadows. With bare hands, she touched one after another. And with each touch, a pulse of light flared, and where a Shadow had lain, now rested an unconscious Arion or supernatural being.

"She's freeing them," Telara whispered. She didn't just know this woman was her mother because of the time Kyler sent her into the past; she knew because she remembered.

Marsella moved with grace, sadness lingering in her every step. She continued her silent work until not a single Shadow remained.

"Are they… all gone?" Telara asked, still scanning the field.

"Not all," Tia said, pointing.

Three small figures still stood at the edge of the battlefield. The mini-Shadows; the girl with floating shadow-pigtails, the thin boy with wicked claws, and a rounder one who waddled slightly. They didn't attack. They only… stared.

Telara turned to Marsella. "Aren't you going to get rid of them?"

Marsella shook her head. "I cannot."

Telara frowned. "Why not?"

"Because they weren't created from my power." Her voice was calm, but weighted.

"Then… whose?" Telara asked.

"You created them, my sweet Tien," Marsella replied gently.

Telara blinked, her heart stuttering in her chest. "What? I —I don't know how to create Shadows. That's not… I couldn't have."

Marsella gave her a look filled with something ancient;

something motherly. "You didn't mean to. But your fear, your pain… it called them. Just as mine once did."

"You created the others?" Mica asked, stunned.

"I thought hydra-bait over there did it," Kull grumbled, jerking a thumb toward Zane.

Zane said nothing, his eyes locked on Marsella. The weight of centuries swam behind them.

Marsella gave him a soft smile. "Zane never created a single Shadow. He let you believe he had, because he was trying to protect me."

Still, Zane said nothing, but he didn't deny it.

"I was the source," Marsella admitted. "It was my grief, my rage, that brought the Shadows into this realm. Larsa imprisoned me within that crystal flower, and siphoned my magic to fuel her own power. She twisted my pain into her weapon."

"Then… we've been fighting your emotions this entire time?" I.Q. asked quietly, his look one of deep thought.

Marsella nodded. "This realm is strange. It responds to deep emotion; love, loss, sorrow, hope. I didn't mean to create them. But they came… anyway."

She looked out across the battlefield where injured Arions were being carried away. "There's more to explain. But for now, our friends need help. We should tend to the wounded, and prepare. Because the final battle is still to come."

Cole frowned. "Wait… that wasn't it?"

Marsella shook her head with a sad smile. "No. This was a storm, but the war still brews. Larsa never controlled the Shadows. She borrowed them. Now that I've reclaimed my power, she'll return to her true plan."

"What plan?" Tia asked warily.

"The death of us… and our children," Kull answered, casting a glare at Zane. "Which makes me wonder why he stayed with her for so long."

"He was trying to bring her down from the inside," Pam

said, stepping forward. Her voice trembled slightly, but her eyes were clear. "He told me everything. He needed to know how she controlled the Shadows before he could stop her. He never knew she was using Marsella's magic."

Zane finally spoke, his voice soft but steady. "I never had anything to do with the Guardians she killed. I only stayed with her… to keep her from killing our children when they were reborn."

Telara held his gaze, her own emotions tangled; but deep down, she believed him. After everything they had seen, after everything they remembered… It made sense now.

"I'm so-" Pam began, her voice cracking.

But Telara rushed forward and pulled her into a tight hug. "No apologies," she whispered. "I'm just glad you're home."

Pam laughed through her tears.

"You can have your command back. Being the leader sucks." They turned to see Gage grinning at them. Pam broke from the Guardians to rush towards Gage who wrapped her in his arms, hugging her tight.

A familiar voice chimed in. "Pammy."

She turned and gave a small smile in greeting. "Claw!"

She pulled the silver necklace from beneath her shirt, the one with the bread and coin charm. "I never got to thank you."

Claw grunted and swung her up in his arms with a grin. "You just did."

The Guardians blinked in surprise. Telara turned to Gage, who only shrugged and grinned. "Long story."

"But it feels like things are finally righting themselves," he added, voice quieter.

Telara nodded, eyes stinging.

"I'm just glad everyone's home," Chance said, voice filled with relief.

"Not everyone," Tia said softly, scanning the crowd. "I don't see my dad."

Marsella walked to her and wrapped her in a warm embrace. "We'll find Zo, Chantria. I promise."

The Guardians moved in, forming a circle around Tia. Telara stepped forward too.

"We'll find him. And Lucius. And then together... we'll finish this. For good."

"Hear, hear!" someone shouted, and soon the battlefield rang with cheers and cries of triumph.

Telara looked around at the sea of faces; friends, family, warriors, and let the warmth of hope fill her chest. They were bruised and battered, but they were alive. United.

They had won the battle.

Now, they needed to rest.

To heal.

To prepare.

She took a deep breath and smiled. "Let's clean up... and see if Lin has dinner ready."

Cole grinned. "Think she made enough for everyone?"

Vanna laughed. "If I know Lin, she's already putting out thirds."

The Guardians, the Paladins, the Arions; everyone, went to work. They tended wounds, cleared rubble, and helped one another stand tall again.

Tomorrow, the next war would come.

But today...

Today was for healing.

And hope.

~

Lucius walked with measured steps through the familiar paths of Sanctuary, his boots stirring dust from the worn stone. The weight of centuries hung on his shoulders, but it no longer crushed him. Hades had released him; Persephone's betrayal had worn down the King of the Underworld. Though Hades still held the crystal, Lucius knew they'd meet again.

But for now, he had a mission.

He glanced toward the Guardians' bungalow, Vanna's tree overlooking Mermaid Lake, eerily silent. Fairy Fields and the Sprite's Domain were quiet too, a rarity in a place that usually hummed with life. All of Sanctuary felt still. Most had gone down to Arcadia, to help their friends in the aftermath of the battle.

He felt a flicker of pride, then quickly admonished himself. "Not here for self-admiration," he murmured.

As he passed the Crystal Caves, he noted the empty carts and pails of crystal essence. He smirked. "Wonder how the gnomes will take it when they realize the crystals don't hold the same importance anymore."

Then he saw him.

At the end of the stone fence, standing motionless as he looked toward the Command Center entrance, was a tall, middle-aged man with dark hair streaked with silver. He carried a presence that tugged at Lucius's memory like a thread unraveling a tapestry. He stood perfectly still, as if the world might shift if he moved.

Lucius stopped a few feet behind him.

"Ira," he said softly.

The figure turned slowly at the sound of his name. The years seemed to melt from his face the moment their eyes met. The once-short hair, peppered with gray, darkened and grew longer. His frame expanded, gaining height and strength until he no longer resembled the awkward figure Telara had once joked looked like Pee-wee Herman.

Lucius's voice was hoarse but steady. "Hello, Zo."

For a heartbeat, nothing moved, just the silence hanging between them like a held breath.

Then Ira's mouth trembled into a small, broken smile.

OTHER BOOKS BY THE AUTHOR

Sanctuary Guardian series reading order:

The Secret Sanctuary

The Town That Time Forgot

The Battle of Sleeping Lady

The Independence Mine Disaster

The Hunter's Betrayal

Haven's Shadow

A Sanctuary Christmas

Echoes of Arcadia

Spider's trilogy in reading order:

Spider's Awakening

Spider's Return

Also from author:

Sanctuary and Friends coloring book

www.ingramcontent.com/pod-product-compliance
Lightning Source LLC
Chambersburg PA
CBHW070459200726
48293CB00007B/2294